焦點英文文法
完全練習

U0033647

Lucy Becker / Carol Frain / Karen Thomas ■ 著　　劉嘉珮 ■ 譯

time clause

present perfect simple tense

direct speech

preposition

either

if

passive form

past tense

of place

must

may adverb of degree

needn't

English grammar

question tag

conditional sentence

superlative adjective

wh-question

modal verb would

the reason why

definite article

defining relative

pronoun

clause

concessive clause

phrasal verb

get sth.

done

關鍵文法解說 + 題型多變的豐富習題
21單元掌握文法重點，由淺入深完全練習
累積文法即戰力，寫出無錯溜英文！

前言

本書以21單元統整文法精要，搭配大量豐富的練習題目，循序漸進打造堅實文法力。
每單元除文法教學說明外，穿插文法延伸補充、文法重點提醒、常見文法問題解惑，
與題型多變的練習題，有助文法吸收、複習與精進，適合用來準備如大考、全民英檢、
多益及托福等各項考試。

每單元分 4 課教學重點

文法解說列點呈現，
更清楚好懂

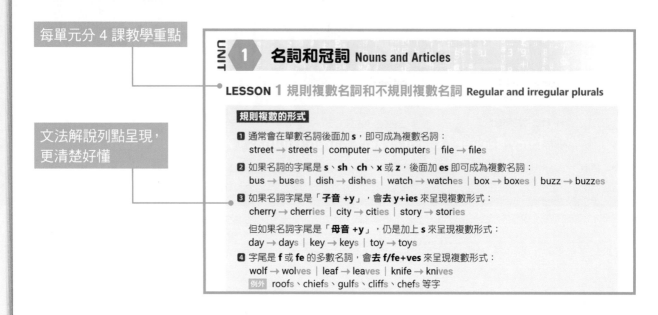

UNIT 1　名詞和冠詞 Nouns and Articles

LESSON 1 規則複數名詞和不規則複數名詞 Regular and irregular plurals

規則複數的形式

❶ 通常會在單數名詞後面加 **s**，即可成為複數名詞：
street → streets｜computer → computers｜file → files

❷ 如果名詞的字尾是 **s**、**sh**、**ch**、**x** 或 **z**，後面加 **es** 即可成為複數名詞：
bus → buses｜dish → dishes｜watch → watches｜box → boxes｜buzz → buzzes

❸ 如果名詞字尾是「**子音 +y**」，會**去 y+ies** 來呈現複數形式：
cherry → cherries｜city → cities｜story → stories

但如果名詞字尾是「**母音 +y**」，仍是加上 **s** 來呈現複數形式：
day → days｜key → keys｜toy → toys

❹ 字尾是 **f** 或 **fe** 的多數名詞，會**去 f/fe+ves** 來呈現複數形式：
wolf → wolves｜leaf → leaves｜knife → knives
例外 roofs、chiefs、gulfs、cliffs、chefs 等字

文法解說下穿插題型
多變的練習題，難度由
淺入深，以 ●（最易）
到 ●●●● 最難）表示

1 請將名詞皆改為複數並填寫至對應欄位。

shelf	boy	strawberry
branch	country	earphone
half	volcano	calf
party	orange	wife

roof	cavity	match
glass	novel	echo
lady	drink	library

fox	life	thief
wish	baby	ray

–s	–es	–ies	–ves

延伸補充

❶ 有些單字源自希臘文或拉丁文，所以複數形式會遵照希臘文或拉丁文的規則來改變：

curriculum → curricula	medium → media	criterion → criteria
phenomenon → phenomena	stimulus → stimuli	antenna （觸角）→ antennae
crisis → crises	thesis → theses	analysis → analyses	hypothesis → hypotheses

延伸補充 介紹課文文法相關的進階知識

當**不可數名詞**以及**抽象名詞**是在說明**一般情況**時，兩者前面均**不可**加定冠詞 **the**！

- I like <u>chocolate</u>.
- <u>Gold</u> is a precious metal.
- <u>Patience</u> is a great virtue.

標示出錯機率高的要點，幫助讀者避免犯錯

FAQ

Q: 我在咖啡廳聽到有人說「**Three coffees, please.**」，如果咖啡是不可數名詞，為什麼這裡是用複數？

A: **coffee** 能當**可數名詞**使用，此時的意思等於「一杯咖啡」，因此比起說 three cups of coffee，可以直接用飲品名稱 coffee 來表達，這樣會比較簡短。

FAQ 以問答方式，解說文法常見疑難雜症，有助加深印象

Focus

注意下列這些名詞在英文裡是**不可數單數**：

furniture	hair	homework
information	money	luggage
news	business	advice

與上述名詞有關的動詞和代名詞，均必須採用**單數形式**：

Is this your luggage?

- Here**'s** my luggage. ~~NOT~~ Here are . . .
- This **is** today's news. ~~NOT~~ These are . . .

Focus 說明相較其他語言，英文文法裡特別的規則，更加釐清文法觀念

每單元後設計一回 Round Up 單元複習，每三單元後一回約八大題的 Revision and Exams 總複習，及一回 Self Check 自我測驗，豐富的練習題讓讀者越寫越上手

ROUND UP 1

1 請使用下列名詞的複數形式來完成句子。

wife half life leaf shelf thief knife loaf

1 Strangely, all three of the actor's former .... are having lunch together in a restaurant.

2 In the first scene of the movie *Autumn in New York*, there are trees with yellow ....

3 The cook in this sushi bar uses very sharp .... to cut the fish.

4 Thousands of .... are at risk in this TV series, but the hero will save everyone.

5 How many .... of bread shall I buy for the party?

6 The books you need are on the two top .... of this bookcase.

7 Cut the peaches into .... and fill them with crumbled macaroon be delicious!

8 I was relaxing in the park when I saw two .... stealing a car.

Revision and Exams 1 (UNITS 1 - 2 - 3)

1 請以 a、an 或 the 來完成下方的電子郵件，並在不需要冠詞的部位，寫上「//」符號。

From: **Asta** astalas@gmail.com
To: **Julie** julieb99@yahoo.com

Hi Julie!
I'm Asta, your new key pal. My teacher gave me your email address. She says we can do an .... this year.
.... an and I live in Vilnius, [1]............ capital city of [2]............ Lithuania. Do you know .... country is? It's in [4]............ north-east of Europe, near [5]............ Russia and .... isn't big, but it's [7]............ interesting country on [8]............
.... at secondary school and I study [10]............
.... languages and I like traveling.

Self Check 1

請選出答案，再至解答頁核對正確與否。

1 There are still some .... on that tree.
Ⓐ leafs Ⓑ leaves Ⓒ leavs

2 The .... are standing near the jewelry store.
Ⓐ policewomens Ⓑ policewoman Ⓒ policewomen

3 Where .... the scissors?

9 I haven't got .... umbrella with me.
Ⓐ an Ⓑ the Ⓒ a

10 Jeff plays .... violin very well.
Ⓐ // Ⓑ a Ⓒ the

11 .... breakfast is served on the terrace.
Ⓐ The Ⓑ A Ⓒ //

12 Spain is in .... south-west of Europe.
Ⓐ the Ⓑ / Ⓒ a

Contents

MAIN ....

UNIT 18 關係子句 Relative Clauses

UNIT 19 直述句和轉述句 Direct Speech and Reported Speech

UNIT 20 連接子句 Connecting Clauses

UNIT 21 語序／片語動詞／構詞方法
Word Order, Phrasal Verbs and Word Formation

附錄 Appendix

Answer Keys　436

名詞和冠詞 Nouns and Articles

LESSON 1 規則複數名詞和不規則複數名詞 Regular and irregular plurals

規則複數的形式

1 通常會在單數名詞後面加 **s**，即可成為複數名詞：

street → street**s** │ computer → computer**s** │ file → file**s**

2 如果名詞的字尾是 **s**、**sh**、**ch**、**x** 或 **z**，後面加 **es** 即可成為複數名詞：

bus → bus**es** │ dish → dish**es** │ watch → watch**es** │ box → box**es** │ buzz → buzz**es**

3 如果名詞字尾是「**子音 +y**」，會**去 y+ies** 來呈現複數形式：

cherry → cherr**ies** │ city → cit**ies** │ story → stor**ies**

但如果名詞字尾是「**母音 +y**」，仍是加上 **s** 來呈現複數形式：

day → day**s** │ key → key**s** │ toy → toy**s**

4 字尾是 **f** 或 **fe** 的多數名詞，會**去 f/fe+ves** 來呈現複數形式：

wolf → wol**ves** │ leaf → lea**ves** │ knife → kni**ves**

例外 roof**s**、chief**s**、gulf**s**、cliff**s**、chef**s** 等字

5 字尾為 **o** 的許多名詞，加上 **es** 即可成為複數形式：

potato → potato**es** │ tomato → tomato**es** │ hero → hero**es**

例外：僅加 s kilo**s**、video**s**、photo**s**、zoo**s**

例外：兩者皆可 volcano**es**/volcano**s**、mango**es**/mango**s**、mosquito**es**/mosquito**s**

---

1 請將名詞皆改為複數並填寫至對應欄位。

shelf	boy	strawberry
branch	country	earphone
half	volcano	calf
party	orange	wife

roof	cavity	match
glass	novel	echo
lady	drink	library

fox	life	thief
wish	baby	ray

−s	−es	−ies	−ves

2 請將句子改寫為複數形式。

1 The school is closed today.　　Schools ....

2 It's an old church.　　They're ....

3 That cliff is dangerous.　　Those ....

4 The shop is open now.　　The ....

5 Where's my key?　　Where ....

6 It's a great city.　　They're ....

7 This story is true.　　These ....

8 A car is parked in the street.　　Two ....

3 請將下列名詞以正確的單數或複數形式呈現，並完成短文。

> wall   singer   shelf   bed   book   poster   actor

In my bedroom there's a bookcase and some [1]........................... which are full of [2]...........................
On the [3]........................... over my [4]........................... there are [5]........................... of my favorite
[6]........................... and [7]........................... .

> armchair   table   sofa   meal   chair

In the living room there's a [8]........................... and two comfortable [9]........................... where we sit
in the evenings. There's also a large [10]........................... and six [11]........................... . We usually have
our [12]........................... there.

4 請將下列名詞以正確的複數形式呈現，並完成短文。

> cherry   strawberry   city   bus   cliff   tomato   potato

I live by the coast in a cottage near some [1]........................... . I have a large garden and I grow my
own fruit and vegetables. I grow [2]........................... and [3]........................... , onions and beans and
I have some fruit trees which produce [4]........................... and apples. I also grow [5]...........................,
which are delicious with sugar and cream. I like living in the country. I don't like [6]...........................
and it is easy to get into town because there are a lot of [7]........................... every day.

不規則複數名詞的形式

❶ 有些名詞具有不規則複數形式：

man → m**e**n	ox → ox**en**	goose → g**ee**se
woman → wom**e**n	tooth → t**ee**th	mouse → m**ice**
child → child**ren**	foot → f**ee**t	louse → l**ice**

penny → pen**ce**
person → people （但是 people 如果是指「人種」，複數形式就要以 peoples 呈現。）

❷ 下列名詞則是以**單數**形式，來同時代表單數和複數的意思：

sheep   fish   deer   dice   means   series   species

5 請將上表名詞以複數形式呈現，來完成句子。

1 Mr. and Mrs. Sherwood have three .... : Gemma, Ian and Matt.

2 That's 85 .... , please.

3 It's a sunny day and lots of .... are having a break from work in the park.

4 Men and .... haven't always had the same rights.

5 .... are big white birds with yellow beaks.

6 .... , rats, and squirrels are all rodents.

7 Buses are a common .... of transportation in towns and cities.

8 We need two .... to play this game.

9 I like the tropical .... in your aquarium.

10 She wears size 10 shoes. She has really big .... !

只有複數形式的名詞

延伸補充

有些名詞只有複數形式，例如：

clothes	goods	binoculars	pajamas	scissors
pants	earnings	contents	vegetables	glasses
shorts	savings	outskirts	remains	surroundings

! 上述名詞一定要搭配**複數動詞**！

"Where **are** the pajamas?" "They**'re** on your bed."

FAQ

Q: 我在音樂雜誌看到這個句子：「**The group are on tour in Italy.**」。可是 group 是單數名詞，為什麼動詞是使用 are 而不是 is？

A: **group** 是**集合名詞**，當代表**一個整體**時可視為**單數**，而當代表**以不同個體結合在一起**的意思時，則視為**複數**。

另外，集合名詞的**代名詞**可以是 **it** 或 **they** 但集合名詞的**所有格形容詞**通常是使用 **their**。

其他集合名詞包括 team、staff、audience、army、family、government、band、class。

Q: 為什麼有人說「**The United States of America is a big country.**」？The United States of America 不應該是複數名詞嗎？

A: 美國（The United States of America）是一個由聯邦州形成的國家，所以是單一實體，為**單數名詞**，後接單數動詞 **is**。

6 請使用 **is** 或 **are** 來完成句子。一題可能有兩個答案。

1 The scissors .... in the top drawer.

2 The Rolling Stones .... playing at the O2 Arena tonight.

3 Your shorts .... in the wardrobe and your new T-shirt .... on your bed.

4 The USA .... in the central part of North America.

5 All my savings .... in a bank account.

6 The government .... debating an important law today.

7 The team .... going to celebrate this evening.

8 Our staff .... all busy at the moment. Please hold.

9 My pajamas .... under the pillow.

10 The United Arab Emirates .... a very rich state.

11 The audience .... mostly students.

12 His team .... in the 1st division.

13 Her glasses .... over there.

14 Their earnings .... enormous!

LESSON 2 可數名詞和不可數名詞 Countable and uncountable nouns

可數名詞和不可數名詞

❶ 可數名詞用於表示可以計算的物體,因此此類名詞會有單數和複數形式:
one car / two cars   one bike / two bikes

❷ 不可數名詞只有單數形式:
bread   rice

❸ 許多不可數名詞會和**食物**與**飲品**有關,像是 water、flour、milk、sugar 等,也會和**材質**有關,如 glass、wood、paper、cotton 等。

❹ 同樣不可數的還有**抽象名詞**:
love   hope   fear   imagination

1 請在可數名詞(**countable noun**)旁寫下 **C**,在不可數名詞(**uncountable noun**)旁寫下 **U**。

wool	lemon	egg	ice	window ....
butter	bottle	beauty	sandwich	snow ....
chair	wine	silver	tea	rain ....
juice	peace	plastic	biscuit	gold ....

請勿於**不可數名詞**前面加上不定冠詞 **a/an**!
不是 a water,而是 **some water**,或是 **a bottle/a glass of water**。
如果要確切表達某種物質的用量,請搭配以下用法:

❶ 丈量單位:a kilo of flour、a pint of beer
❷ 容器名稱:a jar of honey、a cup of tea
❸ 表達整體物品中的一部分:a slice of bread、a bar of chocolate

2 請填入 a、an 或 some。

.... oil	.... bread	.... sweets
.... butter	.... artichoke	.... tomato sauce
.... apple	.... banana	.... mayonnaise
.... onions	.... food	.... sugar

3 請將兩欄文字配對為正確的表達方式。

1 a slice of	**A** salt		1 ....
2 a jar of	**B** tea		2 ....
3 a pinch of	**C** chocolate		3 ....
4 a cup of	**D** cake		4 ....
5 a glass of	**E** sugar		5 ....
6 a bar of	**F** water		6 ....
7 a packet of	**G** yogurt		7 ....
8 a tub of	**H** marmalade		8 ....

4 請將第 2 大題中的名詞填入對應的欄位，再針對各種用量說法，寫下其他食物與飲品的名詞。

a jar of	a bottle of	a kilo of	a bag of	a packet of	a slice of

---

! 當**不可數名詞**以及**抽象名詞**是在說明**一般情況**時，
兩者前面均**不可加定冠詞 the**！

• I like chocolate.
• Gold is a precious metal.
• Patience is a great virtue.

FAQ

Q: 我在咖啡廳聽到有人說
「**Three coffees, please.**」，
如果咖啡是不可數名詞，
為什麼這裡是用複數？

A: **coffee** 能當**可數名詞**使用，此時的意思等於
「一杯咖啡」，因此比起說 three cups of
coffee，可以直接用飲品名稱 coffee 來表達，
這樣會比較簡短。

Focus

注意下列這些名詞在英文裡是**不可數單數**：

furniture	hair	homework
information	money	luggage
news	business	advice

與上述名詞有關的動詞和代名詞，均必須採用
單數形式：

• Here**'s** my luggage. NOT Here ~~are~~ . . .
• This **is** today's news. NOT ~~These are~~ . . .
• How **much** money do you need?
  NOT How ~~many~~ . . . ?
• We haven't got **much** homework today.
  NOT . . . ~~many homeworks~~.
• Her hair **is** beautiful! NOT . . . ~~are~~ beautiful!

Is this your luggage?

5 請以下列名詞搭配正確的 **is** 或 **are** 來完成句子。

> information　news　homework　business　furniture　hair　luggage　teas

1 My .... really long. I want to have it cut.

2 Today's math .... quite difficult. I can't do most of the exercises!

3 The .... they give us when we start college .... always really useful.

4 "Where's your ....?" "It .... at the hotel."

5 The .... on at 10 p.m. There is a report about the situation in Syria.

6 Ikea .... nice and modern.

7 .... good! Our profits are up 10% this year!

8 Here .... two .... and here's the milk.

LESSON 3 不定冠詞 a/an The indefinite article *a/an*

不定冠詞 **a/an** 放於**單數可數名詞**前面，用來描述一件未指定的人事物、舉例事物的類別，或使用在首次提及某事物時，使用 a 和 an 的規則如下：

❶ a 需用於開頭為有聲子音與發音的 **h**、**w** 與 **y** 的單數名詞前面：

a cat | **a** house | **a** window | **a** year

❷ an 需用於開頭為**母音**，或不發音子音 **h** 的名詞前面：

an appointment | **an** only child | **an** English lesson | **an** hour

FAQ

Q: 有哪些單字開頭是不發音的 h 字母？

A: 只有名詞 **hour**、**heir/heiress** 和 **honor**，還有形容詞 **honest** 與其衍生字 **honorable** 和 **honestly** 等。

Q: 為什麼大家都說 **a university**、**a union**、**a European citizen**？這些開頭是母音的字，不是應該使用冠詞 **an** 嗎？

A: 這些字的開頭雖然是 u 和 e，但發音為子音 **[j]**，故應使用冠詞 **a**。

另一方面，看看 an FM radio station 與 an X-ray machine。這裡使用 an 是因為 **f** 的發音是 **[ef]**，**x** 的發音是 **[eks]**。

1 請以 **a** 或 **an** 作答。

1 .... elephant

2 .... yellow car

3 .... interesting book

4 .... window

5 .... horror movie

6 .... uniform

7 .... subway station

8 .... hundred

9 .... art gallery

10 .... hotel

11 .... honest man

12 .... iceberg

13 .... important event

14 .... watch

15 .... unit

16 .... woman

17 .... yacht

18 .... heir

19 .... horse

20 .... hour

21 .... SMS

Focus

不定冠詞可用在以下情境：

1 談論可取用或手上有的物品：
- I've got **an** umbrella. [NOT] I've got ~~the~~ umbrella.
- I haven't got **a** watch. [NOT] I haven't got ~~the~~ watch.

2 用於職業名稱前面：
- My father is **an** engineer. ... I'm **a** teacher.

3 用於疾病前面：
I've got **a** sore throat / **a** cough / **a** temperature / **a** stomachache.

4 表達頻率次數：three times **a** day / once **a** month

5 表達速度：50 km **an** hour

6 表達價格：ten euros **a** kilo

7 表達時間：half **an** hour

8 在 what 和 such 表達感嘆意思的句子裡：
- **What a** day!
- **What a** great champion!
- It's **such a** shame!
- He's **such a** nice boy!

FAQ

Q: 「**a pair of . . .**」和「**a couple of . . .**」有什麼不同？

A: 「**a pair of . . .**」用於表達**兩件可配成一對**的物品，例如 a pair of shoes/glasses/boots 等。

「**a couple of . . .**」則指**兩個或不多的**人事物，例如 a couple of friends、a couple of drinks。

2 請圈出正確的用字。

1 Sorry, I haven't got **a / an / the** pen with me.

2 My brother is **a / an / the** interpreter.

3 What **a / an / the** fantastic match!

4 I've got **a / an / the** bike so I cycle to school every day.

5 A hundred miles **the / a / an** hour! You're going too fast!

6 I've got **the / a / an** very bad headache today.

7 I go running in the park twice **an / a / the** week for half **the / an / a** hour.

8 An apple **the / a / an** day keeps **the / a / an** doctor away!

9 It's such **a / the / an** bad time at the moment. Can I talk to you later?

10 **A / The / An** race is nearly finished.

11 I've got **a / the / an** sore throat.

12 What **a / the / an** great idea!

13 The baby has got **a / the / an** temperature. Let's call the doctor.

14 It was such **an / the / a** amazing concert. You should have come.

15 Have you got **the / a / an** umbrella? It's raining.

16 Those apples are quite expensive — $3 **a / an / the** kilo!

Q: 我可以用 one 來取代冠詞 a/an 嗎？例如說「I've got one cat」會比「I've got a cat」好嗎？

A: 這兩個句子並沒有太大差異，但「I've got a cat」較為普遍，因為 one 多用來回答和**數字**有關的特定問題，例如：

"How many brothers or sisters have you got?"
"I've got one sister and one brother."

另外，副詞 **only** 或 **just** 是表示「**不超過一項的人事物**」、「**只有一個**」的意思。

Q: 為什麼老師會說我寫的「Matthew is a my friend.」是錯的？

A: 因為**冠詞**永遠不能用在**所有格形容詞**的前面。我們可以說「one of my friends」或者「a friend of mine」。如果是複數形式，我們則可以說「some of my friends」。

❗ 千萬不能在**複數名詞**前面使用 **a/an**！
- He's wearing **black pants**. NOT He's wearing a black pants.
- He's got broad **shoulders**. NOT He's got a broad shoulders.

---

3 請使用 a、an 或 one 來完成句子。

1 What .... terrible experience!

2 Just .... bag of chips, please, not two.

3 "How many children have you got?" "I've only got ...., David. He doesn't like being .... only child!"

4 We've got three pets — .... dog and two cats.

5 I need .... pair of jeans and .... couple of white T-shirts.

6 I saw Tom about half .... hour ago.

7 I only need .... apple to make the smoothie.

8 .... of my uncles lives in California.

9 .... good friend of mine won an important prize last week.

10 It was such .... embarrassing situation!

4 請閱讀以下句子。句子如正確，請寫 correct；句子如有錯誤，請訂正。

1 I need a pair of black pants. ....

2 Why don't we go for a walk? It's beautiful day. ....

3 Serena is at home because she's got cough. ....

4 Do you have an high temperature? ....

5 There's a hotel at the end of the road. ....

6 I'm going out with a couple of friends tonight. ....

7 What an horrible day! So many things to do! ....

8 Mike, a your friend's on the phone! ....

9 Sheila has got a brown hair and a brown eyes. ....

10 A friend of mine is waiting for me at the bus stop. ....

5 請以 **a**、**an** 或 **one** 來完成下段短文。

My best friend is [1].......... bank employee. She's [2].......... elegant woman. She's tall and slim with blonde hair and green eyes. She often wears [3].......... pair of pants and [4].......... silk shirt to work. But in her free time she likes to wear casual clothes and [5].......... comfortable pair of sneakers. She's married but, unlike me, she only has [6].......... child while I have three. That's probably why she is much more elegant than me.

LESSON 4 定冠詞 the The definite article "the"

英文只有一個定冠詞，那就是 **the**。然而此冠詞的用法，卻沒有看起來的簡單！

❶ 定冠詞 the 用於**單數和複數名詞前面**，以便準確指示聽者所知道的人事物，或是已經被提及的人事物。請比較差異：

- Take **a** chair.（表示任何一張椅子）
- Put **the** chair in the corner.
  （表示特定的椅子，指在角落那張）
- There's **a** concert at eight o'clock tonight.
- **The** concert starts at eight o'clock.

❷ 定冠詞 the 亦用於下列名詞前方：

❶ 數量上只會有一個的名詞：
- the sun | the moon | the world | the queen | the king | the president
- Peter is **the** new team <u>captain</u>.

❷ 搭配介系詞 of 或 in 的特定名詞：
- **the** inhabitants <u>of</u> Morocco
- I like **the** photos <u>in</u> your blog.

❸ 後方有接 who、which 或 that 關係子句的名詞：
The people <u>who</u> live next door are really nice.

❹ 樂器的名稱：
I can play **the** <u>piano</u> quite well.

❺ 序數詞：
The <u>third</u> day in December is a Monday.

❻ 最高級形容詞：
He's **the** <u>greatest</u> player in the team.

❼ 人種的名稱：
the Chinese | **the** British | **the** French

❽ 當名詞使用的形容詞：
the young | **the** rich

1 請在說明獨特人事物的名詞前方加上 **the**。如非此類名詞，請加上 **a** 或 **an**。

1 ...... equator	**5** ...... Earth	**9** ...... minister	**13** ...... American President
2 ...... bird	**6** ...... insect	**10** ...... Prime Minister	**14** ...... Pope
3 ...... fish	**7** ...... uniform	**11** ...... Pacific Ocean	**15** ...... actress
4 ...... South Pole	**8** ...... Queen	**12** ...... world	**16** ...... North Sea

2 請使用 **a**、**an** 或 **the** 來完成句子。

1 .... capital of Argentina is Buenos Aires. It's .... very big city.

2 They have .... son and .... daughter. .... boy is .... vet and .... girl is .... engineer.

3 Sonia is .... very tall girl. Actually, she's .... tallest girl in .... school.

4 Show me .... video of your wedding. I'd really like to see it.

5 .... sun goes down at about five o'clock in winter.

6 This is .... most important thing of all. Write it down, please.

7 My brother plays .... guitar and .... flute. He's .... very musical person.

8 My birthday's on .... 21st of September.

9 What are .... ingredients in the recipe?

10 .... good friend is someone who can keep .... secret.

FAQ

Q: 我覺得很難判斷何時要用定冠詞 **the**，何時要用不定冠詞 **a/an**。我常常搞混，作業中也常出現這樣的錯誤。

A: 可以試試下面這個方法。想像一下這是一個賓果或樂透遊戲。**a/an** 代表的是抽獎箱裡滾動的球，**the** 就是被抽出的球。

因此：

- **a/an** → 代表許多物品裡的其中一個，也就是未指定、非特定的數字。
- **the** → 代表特定的、有被指定的物體。

另一方面，以複數名詞而言，請謹記以下基本概念：

- **沒有冠詞的複數名詞** → 代表眾物品所屬的一整個類別，也就是一般而論的意思。
- **the + 複數名詞** → 代表精準指定特定物品。

Let's draw a number.

The winning number is . . . twelve!

前面不可加 **the** 的情況：

❶ 指「一般情況」的複數名詞：
- I like **sweets**. NOT ~~the~~ sweets

❷ 抽象名詞：
- **Happiness** is a walk in the park on a sunny day. NOT ~~The~~ happiness is . . .

❸ 正餐的名稱：
- **Lunch** is at one o'clock today. NOT ~~The~~ lunch is . . .

❹ 運動的名稱：
- I play **football** three times a week. NOT I play ~~the~~ football . . .

❺ 學校的科目：
- **Physics** is my favorite subject. NOT ~~The~~ physics is . . .

❻ 所有格形容詞和代名詞：
- our teacher | their lessons | your school
- **Your** sandwiches are ready. NOT ~~The~~ your sandwiches . . .
- "Whose book is it?" "It's **mine**." NOT . . . ~~the~~ mine.

---

3 在必要的位置加上 the 來完成句子。如果是不需要加 the 的位置，請寫上「//」即可。

1 I love .... animals − .... horses are .... my favorite animals.

2 .... pandas that live in .... zoo have a new baby!

3 Mr. Randall is .... new math teacher.

4 Mom likes .... flowers. Let's give her a bunch of .... roses.

5 "Can you play .... guitar?" "No, I can't, but I can play .... drums."

6 .... woman who lives in that house is a famous singer.

7 Are you going to play .... basketball on .... weekend?

8 .... lunch is ready! Everybody go to .... kitchen!

9 "Is this .... your bike?" "No, it isn't; .... mine is blue."

10 .... Italians love .... good food. Some of .... best chefs in .... world are Italian.

> 論及動植物的品種時，我們可以在該**單數**名詞前面加上冠詞 **a/an** 或 **the**，也可以用不需冠詞的**複數**名詞來表達：
>
> **The gazelle** runs very fast. | **A gazelle** runs very fast. | **Gazelles** run very fast.

4 請圈出正確的用字。注意有時答案不只一個。

1 **A / An / The** hyena is **a / an / the** animal that lives in many African countries.

2 **A / An / The** Indian elephant is smaller than **a / an / the** African elephant.

3 **A / An / The** cactus is a plant that grows in the desert.

4 **A / An / The** wombat is **a / an / the** typical Australian animal.

5 **A / An / The** lion is **a / an / the** wild animal.

> 請小心留意**地理名稱**方面的冠詞用法！

The	不需冠詞
山脈（**the** Alps）	單獨的一座山（Mont Blanc）
群島 （**the** Hawaiian Islands）	單獨的島嶼（Malta）
河流（**the** Nile）	湖泊（Lake Superior）
海洋（**the** North Sea、the Pacific Ocean）	城市 （London）

FAQ

Q: 為什麼我們說 Germany、Italy、France，卻要說 the USA？

A: 冠詞僅用於有**複數州份**的國名前面，如 the United States、the Netherlands，或是帶有 **Kingdom**、**Republic** 或 **Federation** 等用字的國名，像是 the United Kingdom、the Czech Republic、the Russian Federation 等。

5 請在必要的位置加上 **the** 來完成句子。如果是不需要加 **the** 的位置，請寫上「///」即可。

1 Paris is .... capital city of .... France.

2 .... highest peaks in .... world are in .... Himalayas.

3 .... USA is between .... Atlantic Ocean to .... east and .... Pacific Ocean to .... west.

4 .... Sardinia and .... Sicily are .... two largest islands in .... Italy.

5 .... Mississippi is .... longest river in .... American continent.

6 "Is Kate from .... Netherlands?" "No, she's from .... Belgium."

7 .... Lake Garda is in .... north-east of .... Italy.

8 .... Thames is the river that runs through .... London.

6 請寫出正確的句子。

1 The mathematics is my favorite subject. ....

2 There's a good movie on at movies this week. ....

3 The quiz starts at the 7:30. ....

4 Jason plays drums. ....

5 Eleanor loves the nature. ....

6 I don't like the tennis. ....

7 These are the your sandwiches. ....

8 Sardinia is the beautiful island. ....

1 請使用下列名詞的複數形式來完成句子。

| wife | half | life | leaf | shelf | thief | knife | loaf |

1 Strangely, all three of the actor's former .... are having lunch together in a restaurant.

2 In the first scene of the movie *Autumn in New York*, there are trees with yellow ....

3 The cook in this sushi bar uses very sharp .... to cut the fish.

4 Thousands of .... are at risk in this TV series, but the hero will save everyone.

5 How many .... of bread shall I buy for the party?

6 The books you need are on the two top .... of this bookcase.

7 Cut the peaches into .... and fill them with crumbled macaroons. The dessert will be delicious!

8 I was relaxing in the park when I saw two .... stealing a car.

2 請使用 **is** 或 **are** 來完成句子。

0 The scissors ....are.... in the drawer.
1 My favorite rock band .... in town.
2 My pajamas .... on the bed.
3 The men .... in the square.
4 All my savings .... in this bank.
5 The goods .... in the truck.
6 The goose .... in the pond.

7 My hair .... too long.
8 The pants .... over there.
9 Your homework .... quite difficult.
10 The information .... very interesting.
11 Where .... my scissors?
12 My luggage .... in the hall.

3 請判斷有底線的單字是單數或複數，單數寫 **S**，複數寫 **P**。

.... **1** There are only three <u>species</u> of big cat in our city zoo.

.... **2** The <u>headquarters</u> of that movie studio are outside our town.

.... **3** Working in a café is a popular <u>means</u> of earning money for students.

.... **4** Are you going to watch the new cartoon <u>series</u> on TV?

.... **5** The actor had an accident at a dangerous <u>crossroads</u>.

.... **6** The <u>media</u> can deeply affect our lives!

延伸補充

❶ 有些單字源自希臘文或拉丁文，所以複數形式會遵照**希臘文或拉丁文**的規則來改變：

curricul**um** → curricul**a**	medi**um** → medi**a**	criteri**on** → criteri**a**
phenomen**on** → phenomen**a**	stimul**us** → stimul**i**	antenna（觸角）→ antenna**e**
cris**is** → cris**es**	thes**is** → thes**es**	analys**is** → analys**es**	hypothes**is** → hypothes**es**

❷ 有些單字雖然同樣出自上述來源，但複數形式還是較常遵照**字尾加 s 或 es** 的英文規則：

| gymnasium → gymnasium**s** | dogma → dogma**s** | genius → genius**es** |

❸ 有些單字則是**兩種變化形式皆可**：

| fungus → fung**i**/fungus**es** | formula → formula**e**/formula**s** | matrix → matr**ices**/matrix**es** |

4 請使用下列名詞的複數形式，來完成短文。所有單字均來自 延伸補充 的內容。

| medium | hypothesis | fungus | analysis | criterion |

Some rare [1]........................... have attacked a precious old painting in the local art gallery. A few famous painters have come up with some different [2]........................... about the cause of this attack. They all agree that further [3]........................... are needed to decide the [4]........................... of the restoration works. All the local [5]........................... are publishing articles about the painting because it is one of the main tourist attractions of the area.

5 請閱讀以下對話，選出正確的選項。

Ann　　How [1] **many** / **much** flour do you need for the cake, Bettie?

Bettie　Not [2] **much** / **many**. Only 300 grams. And we don't need [3] **much** / **many** apples either.

Ann　　How [4] **much** / **many**?

Bettie　Only three. What else do we need?

Ann　　[5] **A** / **An** glass of milk and [6] **some** / **a** jam.

Bettie　Okay. We can start now.

6 請運用以下單字與單位的表達方式，來完成題目。

| a bottle of | a box of | beer | chocolate | a drop of |
| a slice of | a jar of | a cup of | paper | bread |

1　................................ coffee

2　................................ marmalade

3　a sheet of ....

4　a loaf of ....

5　................................ meat

6　................................ Champagne

7　a pint of ....

8　a bar of ....

9　................................ oil

10　................................ cookies

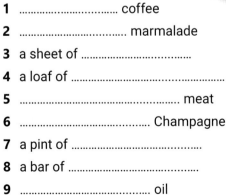

23

有些不可數名詞，能當作具有**複數**形式的**可數名詞**來用，只是**意義會改變**，例如：

business（商業）/ **a** business（一家公司）	hair（頭髮）/ **a** hair（一根髮絲）
paper（紙）/ **a** paper（一份報紙／報告／論文）	damage（損害）/ damage**s**（賠款）

7 請使用題目所提供的單字來完成 Ⓐ、Ⓑ 兩句。如單字為不可數名詞，就以單數形式呈現；如為可數名詞，就以複數形式呈現。

1 experience

Ⓐ This pilot has had a lot of .... flying planes.

Ⓑ I had some wonderful .... in New Zealand last winter.

2 business

Ⓐ Mark has decided to leave his job and go into ....

Ⓑ In spite of the crisis, a number of new .... are setting up in this area.

3 damage

Ⓐ The car driver will have to pay .... of up to £ 5,000 for bumping into the school.

Ⓑ The twister caused quite a lot of ....

4 fish

Ⓐ This .... is delicious. It's cod, isn't it?

Ⓑ The children saw lots of little .... swimming in the shallow water.

5 coffee

Ⓐ "How many .... did we order?" "Four."

Ⓑ "Would you like some more ....?" "No, thanks. I'm fine."

6 glass

Ⓐ The ball hit the window and shattered the .... while the family was having dinner.

Ⓑ There were lots of empty .... on the table after the party.

8 請以 **a**、**an** 或 **the** 來完成以下題目。

1 .... moon	**8** .... Queen	**15** .... actress
2 .... mammal	**9** .... minister	**16** .... EU
3 .... fish	**10** .... Prime Minister	**17** .... sun
4 .... South Pole	**11** .... conference	**18** .... Union Jack
5 .... Earth	**12** .... world	**19** .... yell
6 .... artichoke	**13** .... ostrich	**20** .... yolk
7 .... sky	**14** .... elephant	

9 請使用 a、an 或 the 來完成句子。

1 Take a chair. Take .... red chair near .... desk.

2 .... capital of Morocco is Rabat. It's .... big city.

3 He has two pets, ... rabbit and .... hamster. .... rabbit is white and .... hamster is brown.

4 Sonia is .... tallest girl in our class.

5 The Coliseum is .... biggest amphitheater I've ever seen.

6 .... sun sets at about five in winter.

7 There's .... full moon tonight.

8 I really like .... cookies your mother has made.

延伸補充

以下情況亦使用定冠詞 the：

❶ 表示一對夫妻或一整個家庭，此時 the 後要加姓氏的複數：
- **the** Wades　　• **the** Baileys

❷ 表示不同組織或種類的縮寫：
- **the** WWF (World Wildlife Fund)
- **the** UN (United Nations)
- **the** EU (European Union)

❸ 放在場所名詞前，此時作為行為動詞前往的地方，或狀態動詞的直接受詞：
- They usually go to **the** seaside in summer.
- Why don't we buy a cottage in **the** mountains?
- I love spending my free time in **the** garden.
- We always walk to **the** office together.

場所名詞如：garden、park、cinema/movies、theater、mountains、country/countryside、seaside、office、swimming pool 等。

Reflecting on grammar

請研讀文法規則，再判斷以下說法是否正確。

		True	False
1	所有單數名詞在後方加 s 即可成為複數名詞。		
2	有些名詞沒有單數形式。		
3	所有名詞改為複數時都依不同的規則。		
4	抽象名詞均不可數。		
5	luggage 或 money 等名詞，需以複數形式呈現。		
6	yacht 或 university 等開頭發音為 [j] 的單字，前面使用的冠詞為 an。		
7	a pair of 與 a couple of 的用法並無差異。		
8	用以表示「一般情況」的複數名詞，前面不可使用定冠詞。		
9	所有格形容詞前面一定要有冠詞。		
10	湖泊名稱前面不能使用冠詞。		

UNIT 2 人稱代名詞和 be 動詞 Personal Pronouns and Verb *be*

LESSON 1 主格代名詞 Subject pronouns

人稱代名詞的主格形式

單數	I	you	he	she	it
複數	we	you	they		

❶ **he** 用於替代**男性**的名稱：my brother / Harry → **he**

❷ **she** 用以替代**女性**的名稱：my sister / Ellen → **she**

❸ **it** 用以替代**事物或動物**的名稱：my diary / the rabbit → **it**

❹ **they** 用以替代**人事物或動物**的**複數**名詞：
the children / Tony and Jo / the books / my dogs → **they**

FAQ

Q: 在講我自己的狗時要使用代名詞 it 比較好，還是要因為是公狗而用 he 比較好？

A: 一般來說，我們會視**寵物的性別**而使用男生的代名詞 he 或女生的代名詞 she。例如：「I've got a cat. She's black and white.」。另一方面，如果我們不清楚動物的性別，我們會使用中性的代名詞 it。

Q: 我經介紹結識某人時，說了「Nice to meet you.」（很高興認識你），我直接用平語（你）稱呼對方。難道我不需使用敬語（您）嗎？

A: 不用，因為**英文沒有敬語的文法**。無論是與朋友還是不熟的人對話，都是直接用代名詞 you。

1 請閱讀以下句子，圈出正確的代名詞。

1 Rebecca is French. **He / She** comes from Paris.

2 Robert is my new classmate. **She / He** is very nice.

3 Tina and I are best friends. **We / They** are always together.

4 Sam and Mark are very tall. **You / They** play in the basketball team.

5 Do **you / we** like my jacket? **She / It** is new and **it / she** was a real bargain.

6 You and Emma go to the same school. Are **you / we** in the same class, too?

7 These are good history books. **It / They** are about Napoleon.

8 Here's the article about cyberbullying. **He / It** is very interesting.

9 Carol and Sue live next door to each other. **They / We** both work at the same supermarket.

10 Have a look at our online catalog, Dave. **You / It** will find it very useful.

代名詞 it

代名詞 **it** 是英文的常用字。可用於許多非人稱的表達方式，例如：

- **It**'s all right / okay.
- **It**'s late/early.
- **It**'s time to go to bed.
- **It**'s great to be here!
- **It** is also used in the following cases:

其他常用的情況如下：

❶ 表達星期幾、日期與時間：• **It**'s Tuesday, the 3rd of February. • **It**'s four o'clock.
❷ 表達天氣氣候：• **It**'s raining. • **It**'s cold.
❸ 表達距離和旅行時間：• **It**'s 150 km from here. • **It** takes two hours.
❹ 表達價格：• **It**'s three pounds fifty.
❺ 接電話時的回話方式，或是應門的方式：
  • **It**'s Miss Collins speaking. • "Who is **it**?" "**It**'s me, Sarah."
❻ 用來詢問某人是誰的時候：• "Who's that over there?" "**It**'s Mr. Jones, my art teacher."

Focus

❶ 英文的句型必須要有主詞，而最常見的主詞就是**名詞**或**人稱代名詞**：
  • **My teacher**'s nice. • **I**'m tired. • **You**'re late. • **He**'s happy.

❷ 以 **and**、**but** 或 **or** 構成的對等子句裡，如果**主格代名詞**與主要子句裡的**主詞**相同，即可**省略**。
  • We usually watch TV **or** (we) listen to music after dinner.
  • I meet my friends **and** (I) go to the movies on Sundays.

❗ 名詞後面千萬不能加上代名詞——代名詞的功能就是取代名詞，所以只能擇一使用！
  • My mom's at home now. NOT ~~My mom she's~~ at home now.
  • Simon and Fiona are cousins. NOT ~~Simon and Fiona they're~~ cousins.

---

2 請使用人稱代名詞來完成句子。

1 .... is a beautiful girl. And .... is very clever, too.

2 .... are Uncle George and Aunt Carol. .... live in Chester.

3 .... am a very sensitive person. .... can't stand arrogant people.

4 Karl and Thomas are brothers. .... are twins.

5 Bob, come on! .... are late for school as usual.

6 I love designer clothes, but .... are so expensive!

7 This is my friend Tom. .... is staying with us for the weekend.

8 My sister and I get on very well. .... help each other a lot.

9 Pleased to meet you, Ms. Blake. .... must be the new web designer, right?

10 Meet Morris, our receptionist. .... will help you during your internship.

11 Have you seen Suzie, my cat? .... is missing again!

12 Wendy and Mike, can .... organize the tickets for the concert, please?

13 My brother and I are very alike, but .... don't get on very well.

14 "Kate and I won the dance competition last night!" "That's wonderful, ...'re such great dancers!"

3 請將問句和答句配對。

..... **1** How much is a Coke?

..... **2** How far is it to the Lake District?

..... **3** How long does it take to get there?

..... **4** What's the time, please?

..... **5** What day is it today?

..... **6** How about going to the seaside?

..... **7** What's the weather like?

..... **8** Who's that over there?

A It's Thursday, the 11th of May.

B It's hot and sunny.

C I think that's a great idea!

D It's one dollar thirty cents.

E It's a friend of mine.

F It's a quarter past nine.

G It takes about an hour.

H It's about two hundred miles.

4 請用括號標出可以省略的代名詞，並將用法錯誤的代名詞畫叉（✗）。

0 We start work at 9 a.m. and (we) finish at 5:30 p.m.

1 My dad he always gets back home very late.

2 Ann likes cooking but she hates cleaning the kitchen.

3 On Saturdays they go shopping or they see their friends.

4 John and Kylie they have a lot of common interests.

5 Marion plays computer games or she reads a book in her spare time.

6 The movie it starts at 8:30 and it ends at eleven o'clock.

7 I love Japanese food but I don't like Indian food. It's too hot and spicy.

8 Mr. Ross leaves home at 7:30 every morning and he takes a bus to his office.

9 Jason he is late as usual.

10 Karen doesn't play the piano but she sings beautifully.

11 The children they go to the playground every afternoon.

5 請圈出正確的用字。

1 "What's the weather like?"
"**He's** / **It's** cold and cloudy."

2 "How much **'s** / **is** that jacket?" "It's £27."

3 **You're** / **They're** Mr. Ross, right?

4 "What day is it today?" "**It's** / **Is** Friday."

5 "**Is** / **Who's** that boy over there?"
"**Is** / **He's** Tom, the new student."

6 "You are late as usual!"
"That's not true. **I'm** / **You're** never late!"

LESSON 2 be 動詞 Verb *be*

→ 圖解請見 P. 404

be 動詞：肯定句

be 動詞有三種形式：am、is、are。
有完整形式也有縮讀形式。

完整形式	縮讀形式
I am	I'm
You are	You're
He is	He's
She is	She's
It is	It's
We are	We're
You are	You're
They are	They're

It's so cute!

縮讀形式除了常用在口語和書寫上，也能用在非 s 結尾的單數名詞主詞後，如：
• **Kate's** a nice girl. •• My **dad's** a great cook!

1 請使用正確的 **be** 動詞形式來造句。

1 Camilla / a nice old lady ....

2 Brian / thirsty ....

3 Jack and Debbie / our next-door neighbors ....

4 The dog / outside in the garden ....

5 Mark and I / cousins ....

6 My parents / on vacation in Spain ....

7 I / very tired tonight ....

8 You / really funny ....

2 請盡可能使用縮讀形式的 **am/is/are** 來完成句子。記得如果主詞是以兩個名詞或一個複數名詞構成，即不可使用縮讀形式。

1 You .... 16 years old, but you look younger.

2 It .... a trendy jacket.

3 Tom and Jerry .... my cats.

4 She .... my younger sister, Lucy.

5 He .... a successful businessman.

6 Mark .... a very young musician. He .... only 11.

7 They .... from Scotland, but they live in London.

8 We .... here on vacation.

9 I .... interested in modern art.

10 My friends .... crazy!

3 請運用以下單字或片語來完成句子。

| thirsty   sleepy   hot   in a hurry   right   scared   cold   hungry |

1 I'm .... Can I have some water, please?

2 Why are you running? You're always ....

3 You're .... This is the best place to be on vacation!

4 I'm .... Close the window, please.

5 I'm .... of spiders! Especially the black hairy ones.

6 I'm very .... Can I have something to eat?

7 I'm so ....! It must be the jetlag.

8 It's .... in here. Turn the heater off.

4 請使用正確的 **be** 動詞形式來完成短文。

Hi, my name [1].............. Sam. I [2].............. a student at Bath University.
My brother [3].............. here too. We [4].............. both sportsmen. He [5].............. good at
swimming and I [6].............. good at running. Bath [7].............. a great place to study.
The campus [8].............. five minutes away from the center by bus. My parents
[9].............. from near here, so they [10].............. often here to visit us!

完整形式	縮讀形式
I am not	I'm not
You are not	You aren't
He is not	He isn't
She is not	She isn't
It is not	It isn't
We are not	We aren't
You are not	You aren't
They are not	They aren't

This isn't my dog.

> 縮讀形式同樣常見於**否定句**。如果要加強語氣，我們可以使用「you're not」、「he's not」、「we're not」等形式，但注意沒有「I amn't」這個說法。
> 看看例句：「I think Roland's French.」「**He's not** French; he's Belgian!」。

5 請將句子改寫為含縮讀形式的否定句。

1 We're ready for the test. ....
2 They're at home now. ....
3 It's too late! ....
4 Aman is at school today. ....
5 I'm afraid of the dark. ....
6 She's 17 years old. ....
7 My parents are at work. ....
8 I'm very good at math. ....

6 請完成句子，盡可能使用縮讀形式的 be 動詞。

1 You .... a bad player. You can play quite well!
2 Your eyes .... brown. They're green.
3 I .... on a diet. I want to lose some weight.
4 We .... friends and we go to the same school.
5 Claire and I .... sisters. We're cousins.
6 Karen .... British. She's Australian.
7 Mr. and Mrs. Taylor .... from York. They're from Leeds.
8 These jeans aren't blue. They .... black.

7 請以肯定或否定的 be 動詞來完成短文。

Sam and Phil [1]............. students at a comprehensive school in London. Sam [2]............. 16 and Phil [3]............. 17. They live in London, but they [4]............. English. Sam [5]............. Irish, and Phil [6]............. from Scotland. I [7]............. a good friend of Sam and Phil's even if I [8]............. at their school. We often see each other in the afternoon after school because we [9]............. in the same football team.

be 動詞：疑問句與簡答句

問句裡的 be 動詞必須放在主詞前面。

	Are you . . . ?	Is he/she/it . . . ?	Are you/we/they . . . ?
簡答句	Yes, I am.	Yes, he/she/it is.	Yes, we/you/they are.
疑問句	No, I'm not.	No, he/she/it isn't.	No, we/you/they aren't.

簡答句句型

Yes, + 代名詞 + am/is/are.
No, + 代名詞 + 'm not / isn't / aren't.

肯定答句裡，be 動詞會以完整形式來呈現，**否定答句**則通常會使用縮讀形式：

- "Is your room on the first floor?" "**Yes, it is.**" NOT Yes, it's.
- "Is it a large room?" "**No, it isn't.** It's quite small."

請注意，亦可使用「No, he/she/it's not.」以及「No, we/you/they're not.」。

否定問句

Aren't we/you/they . . . ?	• "**Aren't you** happy?" "Yes, I am!" （「你難道不開心嗎？」「我很開心！」）
Isn't he/she/it . . . ?	• "**Isn't it** a good idea?" "No, it isn't." （「這不是個好主意嗎？」「不，這不是。」）

請注意「**Am I not** . . . ?」沒有縮讀形式，如：

「**Am I not** good?」（也可以用「**Aren't I** good?」）「Oh, yes, you're very good!」

⑧ 請填入 be 動詞來完成問句。

1 .... Sara at school today?

2 .... they on vacation on Tuesday?

3 .... we here tomorrow?

4 .... I late?

5 .... she at the dentist's?

6 .... you American?

⑨ 請完成問句和簡答句。

1 "...... they at home today?" "No, they ...."

2 "...... she here tomorrow?" "Yes, she ...."

3 "...... we happy?" "No, we .... !"

4 "...... I part of this class?" "Yes, you ...."

5 "...... he out?" "Yes, he ...."

6 "...... it red?" "No, it ...."

⑩ 請使用提示用詞和 be 動詞，寫出肯定問句或否定問句，再寫下簡答句。

0 your son / a teenager → Is your son a teenager?

No, he isn't . He's 22 years old.

1 Matthew / Susan's cousin → .... ?

Yes, ...

2 he / not / a good singer → .... ?

Yes, ...

3 your children / at school / today → .... ?

No, ... They're on vacation.

4 your sister's name / Claire → .... ?

Yes, ...

5 Chris and Daniel / twins → .... ?

No, ... Chris is older than Daniel.

6 Bob and Edward / not / good friends → .... ?

Yes, ...

11 請依照答句內容，寫出合適的問句。

1 "..?"

"No, you aren't short, Ann.
You're quite tall."

2 ".. in here?"

"No, I'm quite cold. Close the
window, please."

3 "..
of the dark?"

"Yes, quite. Switch on the light, please."

4 "..?"

"No, my sister is terrible at math."

5 "..?"

"Sisters? No, Claire and I are cousins."

6 "..?"

"On the first floor? No, Peter's office
is on the second one."

7 "..?"

"Mark? No, John has got a sister.
He hasn't got any brothers."

8 "..?"

"Yes, very. Can I have a sandwich, please?"

LESSON 3 There is / There are There is / There are

→ 圖解請見P. 414

There is / There are

肯定句	**There is** a/an/some . . .	**There are** some . . .
否定句	**There isn't** a/an/any . . .	**There aren't** any . . .
疑問句	**Is there** a/an/any . . . ?	**Are there** any . . . ?
簡答句	Yes, **there is.** No, **there isn't.**	Yes, **there are.** No, **there aren't.**

❶ 當我們**第一次介紹**某事物的存在時，會使用 **There is/are** 的句型，並將真正的主詞放在 be 動詞後面：<u>There is a new restaurant in Hill Street.</u> **NOT** A~~ new restaurant~~ is in Hill Street.

❷ **There is** （縮寫為 There's）後面可以接**單數可數**名詞，或是**不可數**名詞：
• There's <u>a party</u> tomorrow. • There's <u>some cheese</u> in the fridge.

❸ **There are** 後面則必須接**複數**名詞：There are <u>some photos</u> of the concert on my blog.

FAQ

Q: 我聽過人家說：「**In my bedroom, there's a wardrobe, a desk and two chairs.**」為什麼是用「**there's**」而不是「**there are**」？不是陳述了好幾樣東西嗎？

A: 當要表達一長串事物時，如果第一個物品是**單數**，我們開頭會先用 **There is**，就像你聽到的句子一樣。如果第一個物品是**複數**，我們就會以 **There are** 開頭，例如「**There are two chairs, a desk and a wardrobe.**」。

Here/There

❶ **Here** 是代表場所的副詞，意指「在這個場所裡」，用於表示**靠近**講者的某物或某人：
- Here's your seat. / Here are your bags.
- Where's my pen? Oh, here it is.

❷ 我們將某物交給某人的時候，會使用「**Here you are**」或「**Here's . . .**」的表達方式：
- Here's your change.   • "Can I have the bill, please?" "Sure. Here you are."

❸ **There** 一樣是代表場所的副詞，但用於表示和講者**有段距離**的某物或某人：
- There's your car!
- Where's David? Oh, there he is!

如果要表達的某人或某物是**名詞**，就必須放在句中動詞的**後面**：
- Here **are** your keys.

但如果是**代名詞**，則要放在動詞的**前面**：
- Here they **are**.

UNIT

2

人稱代名詞和 be 動詞

1 請使用 there's、there are、there isn't 或 there aren't 來完成句子。

1 .... a very good movie on Channel 5 tonight. I want to see it.

2 .... a washing machine in my apartment, but there's a launderette nearby.

3 .... a sofa and two armchairs in the living room.

4 .... two beds and two desks in our bedroom.

5 .... any milk in the fridge. We must get some.

6 .... any glasses in the closet. They're all in the dishwasher.

7 .... a large living room, but .... a study in my house.

8 .... any plants on the balcony. I want to buy some.

2 請先使用 Is there 或 Are there 完成問句，再完成簡答句。

0 .....Is there........ a park near your house?   Yes, ...there is....... . It's just opposite my house.

1 .... any parks around here?   Yes, ... There's one over there.

2 .... a station in your village?   No, ... But there's a good bus service.

3 .... any ATMs in the town center?   Yes, ... Three or four.

4 .... a supermarket near here?   No, ... , but there are some shops.

5 .... a hospital around here?   Yes, ... The Milford Hospital.

6 .... any restaurants nearby?   No, ... Just a couple of pubs.

3 請使用 here 或 there 完成句子。

1 Where's the car? Oh, ... it is — next to that red car.

2 Where are my keys? Ah, ... they are — in the bottom of my bag.

3 Where's Mark? Ah, ... he is — I can see him outside.

4 Thanks for buying my lunch. ....'s the money.

5 You're at the front — ah, ...'s your seat.

6 "Can I have the results?" "Sure, ... you are."

33

1 如需詢問某人在何處，可以說：「Is John **here**?」（表示 John 比較靠近講者）或者
「Is John **there**?」（表示 John 離講者有段距離），而不是「Is there John?」。
回答方式則為：Yes, he is. / No, he isn't.
請同時參考："Are your parents there?" "No, they aren't. They're out."

2 如果想詢問有多少人在場，可問「How many of you are **there**?」，回答方式則為
「**There are** four of us.」或「**There's** four of us.」，注意不是「We are in four.」。
相關問法還有：How many of us/them are there?

4 請畫底線在句中有誤處，並訂正為正確句子。

0 <u>Is here</u> Simon?　　　　　　　　　　　　　*Is Simon here?*

1 Here's a great match tomorrow.　　　　...

2 There are one table and four chairs in the kitchen.　...

3 "Is there your brother?" "No, he's at work."　...

4 "There is a room for tonight?" "Yes, there is."　...

5 Here it is your bill.　　　　　　　　...

6 How many of you there are?　　　　...

7 There are any tickets left?　　　　　...

8 There's two bags on the table.　　　...

LESSON 4 疑問詞 Question words

疑問詞（或稱 **Wh** 疑問詞）均需放在**句首**。身兼**代名詞**、**副詞**和**疑問形容詞**的主要疑問詞如下：

詢問類型

Who? 詢問人物	**When?** 詢問時間	**Which?** 詢問選擇
What? 詢問事物	**Why?** 詢問原因	**Whose?** 詢問何者持有該物
Where? 詢問場所		

1 what 可作為後接名詞的代名詞或形容詞：
- **What**'s your email address?
- **What** kind of music do you like?

2 which 可作為代名詞或形容詞。如果**選擇有限**，我們通常會使用 **which**；**選擇範圍較廣**的話，我們會使用 **what**：
- **Which** subject do you prefer? Math or science?（意指在數學與科學中選一）
- **What**'s your favorite subject?（意指在所有學科裡做選擇）

Focus

切記！回答 **why** 問句時必須使用 **because**。
- "**Why** are you late?" "**Because** the bus was late."

1 請將問句和答句配對。

..... **1** What are you buying?

..... **2** Where are they going?

..... **3** Who's that boy?

..... **4** When are you coming to see me?

..... **5** Which one is your bicycle?

..... **6** Why are you so late?

..... **7** Which of these jackets do you prefer?

..... **8** Whose book is this?

A He's Paul, our new classmate.

B Because I missed the bus.

C The red one over there. It's new.

D It's my book.

E Some food and drinks for the party.

F I like the red leather one.

G Maybe next Saturday.

H They're going home.

「How . . . ?」疑問詞

另一種疑問副詞就是 how。how 用於表達其他類型的各種問句,例如:

❶ 詢問不可數名詞的數量或價格 → How much?

❷ 詢問可數名詞的數量 → How many?

❸ 詢問年齡 → How old?

❹ 詢問進行某事所需要的時間長短 → How long?

❺ 詢問距離 → How far?

❻ 詢問頻率次數 → How often?

2 請以合適的疑問詞完成問句。

1 .... is your English teacher?　　I think she's nearly 60.

2 .... does it take you to go home?　　About 15 minutes.

3 .... students are in your class?　　Twenty-five.

4 .... is this skirt?　　It's $25.

5 .... are you so unhappy?　　Because I got a D in math.

6 .... is your school from here?　　It's about 500 meters.

7 .... is your birthday?　　It's on January 5th.

8 .... are you and your family?　　We're all very well, thanks.

9 .... is Mr. Smith?　　He's in his office.

10 .... do you practice?　　Three times a week.

> **!** Wh 疑問詞一定要放在問句的**句首**。

Focus

如果英文問句裡有**介系詞**,通常會放在問句的**句尾**:

- Who is this **for**?
- What is it **about**?
- Who are you going on vacation **with**?
- Which computer are you working **on**?
- Where do they come **from**?

FAQ

Q: 有人曾問我：「What's your school like?」我回答：「I like it very much.」後來我恍然大悟，原來這個問句不是在問「你喜歡你的學校嗎？」，而是在籠統地問學校的概況。但為什麼問句不是用「How is your school?」表達？

A: 「**What . . . like?**」通常希望答者能**說明**問句裡提及的人事物的情況，此時的 like 是當介系詞。所以你可以回答如：「It's a big school.」、「It's old/modern.」等。

這類問句的另一個例子就是「What's your family like?」，此時可以回答「It's a big family – two brothers and a sister.」。而若問「**How is your family?**」則是在關心你家人**健康狀態**，回應方式則可為：「We're all very well, thanks.」。

3 請使用提示用詞先寫出問句，再與正確的答句配對。

1 like / what's / house / your/?

....

2 you / talking / to / are / who / ?

....

3 the / what's / like / weather / ?

....

4 is / how / now / Peter / ?

....

5 your / like / sister / what's / ?

....

6 from / are / you / where / ?

....

7 are / talking / about / you / what / ?

....

8 is / this / for / present / who / ?

....

A It's very cloudy. It's going to rain.

B He's much better, thanks.

C She's quite tall and she's got long hair.

D It's a small semi-detached house.

E We're from Mexico.

F We're talking about music.

G It's for Mom. It's her birthday tomorrow.

H I'm talking to Grandma.

1 .....   2 .....   3 .....   4 .....   5 .....   6 .....   7 .....   8 .....

4 請根據答句內容，寫出合適的問句。

1 ....? My family's pretty small. Only me and my mom.

2 ....? John is only at home in the afternoons.

3 ....? The party is at the youth club.

4 ....? Mr. Blackwell? He's my ICT teacher.

5 ....? My favorite food is pizza.

6 ....? It's 347 998532.

7 ....? Silvia's from Rome.

8 ....? There are twenty people.

9 ....? I think I've got about $20 in my wallet.

10 ....? Carol? She prefers the black car.

尺寸方面的疑問詞

How high? 詢問**從上到下的距離**，如山脈、書架等高度

How wide? 詢問**兩側的距離**，如道路、湖泊的寬度

How tall? 詢問人物、圓柱體、狹長物體、建築物和樹木的**高度**

How long? 詢問**從起點到終點的距離**

How deep? 詢問表面至底部的距離，如海洋、湖泊等**深度**

How big? 詢問體積或面積的**大小**

Focus

以英文回答上述問句時，要先表達**數字**再接**形容詞**：

- "How tall is Brian?" "He's **1.70** m **tall**."
- "How long is the Eurotunnel?" "It's **50** km **long**."

切記！「How long?」也能用以詢問**時間長短**：

- **How long** does it take to get to your house?

5 請重新排序單字，寫出正確的問句。

1 Everest / is / Mount / high / How / ? ....

2 long/is / River / How / Mississippi / the / ? ....

3 Ness / deep / How / Loch / is / ? ....

4 of / is / Wight / big / the / Isle / How / ? ....

5 brother / How / is / your / tall / ? ....

6 this / is / wide / How / table / ? ....

6 請將第 5 大題 **1–6** 的問句與下方 **A–F** 的答句配對。

1 .....   **A** It's 80 cm wide.

2 .....   **B** It covers an area of 380 km², nearly 150 square miles.

3 .....   **C** Its deepest point is 230 m (755 ft).

4 .....   **D** He's nearly 2 m tall.

5 .....   **E** It's approximately 3,730 km long (2,320 miles).

6 .....   **F** It's 8,848 m (29,029 ft). It's the world's highest mountain.

ROUND UP 2

1 請改寫句子，用代名詞取代畫底線的名詞。

1 <u>Phil and Josh</u> are both from Korea. ....

2 <u>Silvia</u> is 16 years old. ....

3 <u>East Side Comprehensive</u> is a big school. ....

4 <u>Peter</u> is Swedish. ....

5 <u>Jim and I</u> are friends. ....

2 請以合適的主格代名詞完成對話。

A Look at that girl! What's her name?

B [1]...............'s Erica.

A Erica? Is [2]............... English?

B No, [3]...............'s Italian. [4]...............'s here with a group of Italian students on a school exchange visit.

A Are [5]............... here on a European project?

B Yes. [6]...............'s Erasmus Plus.

A Are [7]............... part of it?

B No. [8]............... 'm not. [9]............... 'm too young. [10]............... 's for people in grade 11.

3 請使用 there is/are 改寫句子。

0 A lot of people are on the beach today. ....There are a lot of people on the beach today.....

1 A lamp and a book are on my bedside table. ....

2 Three cans of orangeade are in the fridge. ....

3 A new boy is in my class this year. ....

4 A lot of books are in your rucksack! ....

5 Only 12 students are in the class today. ....

6 A lot of good songs are on my MP3 player. ....

4 請以正確的 be 動詞肯定句或否定句來完成短文。

Sam and Thomas [1]............... colleagues at Barkley's Bank in Newcastle. Sam [2]............... 26 and Thomas [3]............... 30. They live in Newcastle now, but they [4]............... English. Thomas [5]............... Scottish and Sam [6]............... American.

I [7]............... a good friend of Sam's even if I [8]............... in the same office. I work as an accountant for a big kitchenware factory just outside Newcastle. We often meet on the weekend because we [9]............... in the same five-a-side football team.

5 請使用正確的 be 動詞形式來完成短文，並於必要位置加上主格代名詞。

Having a family around you [1]............... a wonderful feeling. I think [2]............... very important to [3]............... with your family. The family [4]............... the center of your life. The people in your family [5]............... always there to help you if [6]............... in trouble and to share good times when [7]............... happy. Your mother [8]............... probably the person who [9]............... closest to you when [10]............... small, but your brothers and sisters [11]............... more important when you get older.

6 以下每個句子均有一個文法錯誤，請訂正並寫出正確句子。

1 Susan and I am students in this school.

....

2 Janet is 15 and her twin brothers is 20.

....

3 – Who are that man?   ....

– She's my uncle.   ....

4 – Is you a member of the drama club?   ....

– Yes, I'm.   ....

5 Thomas and his friend is taking part in the school tennis tournament.

....

6 The student's room are on the first floor.

....

7 I know that policeman. She's a friend of my brother's.

....

8 Is we going to the movies tonight?

....

7 請填空單字以完成對話。

At the restaurant

Man Is ⁰....there.... a table for two, please?

Waiter Yes, sir. ¹......................... one, by the window.

Man Can we see the menu, please?

Waiter Of course. Here ²......................... .

Man ³......................... any vegetarian dishes?

Waiter Yes, there ⁴......................... some, on page 3.

Man Great! Umm . . . I'll have the couscous with vegetables.

Woman And I'll have the tomato soup.

Waiter Okay, thank you.

(A few minutes later)

Waiter ⁵......................... you are, couscous with vegetables and your soup, madam.

Man This is delicious! What about your soup?

Woman ⁶......................... very nice.

Man Would you like anything else?

Woman No, I'm fine.

Man Okay. Can we have the bill, please?

Waiter Sure, ⁷......................... your bill. ⁸......................... $30.25.

Man Here ⁹......................... . Thank you.

Waiter And ¹⁰......................... your change, sir.

8 請填空以完成對話。

1 "Is your father at home in the evenings?" "Yes, ... is."

2 ".............. Mrs. Basset your math teacher?" "No, she .... She's my history teacher."

3 "How .... is your home from the town center?" "About 2 km."

4 "Why .... Marion at school today?" "Because .... is ill."

5 "Who's that girl?" ".............. my sister Tricia."

6 ".............. you at home tonight?" "No, I'm ...."

7 "What's your town ....?" "It's small but pretty."

8 "..............'s your brother?" "He's fine, thank you."

延伸補充

it's 和 that's 的差異如下。「**It's . . .**」通常用以**告知新訊**，而「**That's . . .**」則是針對**他人說過的事物表達意見**，其中的 that 其實是代指他人剛剛說過的事物：

- **It's** time to go.（宣告談話對象所不知道的事物）
- So it's time to go. **That's** too bad!（That 意指上一句話裡的「必須離開」）
- A holiday in Greece? **That's** great!

---

9 請將 1–6 的句子和 A–F 的句子配對。

..... 1 I'm eating lots of vegetables these days.

..... 2 I'm taking a short break.

..... 3 Look! That's Henry's mom!

..... 4 It's only two degrees!

..... 5 Where's Marcia's house?

..... 6 It costs $40.

A That's good! You need one.

B That's expensive!

C It's a long way from here.

D That's good for you!

E That's cold!

F No, it's his sister!

---

10 請使用包括提示用詞在內的二至五個單字，來完成意義相近的句子。（注意不能變更提示用詞）

1 In my opinion, inviting Susan to the party is not a good idea.

IT   In my opinion, ... idea to invite Susan to the party.

2 I think arguing with your family is very upsetting.

TO   I think .... argue with your family.

3 That's Mom's favorite vase, so don't break it!

BECAUSE   Don't break that vase .... favorite!

4 Yes, I agree that going to the movies this evening is a good idea.

OKAY   Yes, ... me if we go to the movies this evening.

5 Mom says eating fish is good for me.

IT   Mom says .... to eat fish.

6 What you just said was the nicest thing anyone's ever said to me!

THAT   .... anyone's ever said to me!

11 請使用 it's 或 that's 來完成對話。

1 "Who's on the phone?"

".............. Peter."

2 ".............. very cold in this room."

"Oh, dear. .... too bad. There's a meeting in here in a quarter of an hour."

3 "Shall we eat out tonight?"

".............. a good idea."

4 "Shall we go?"

"No, ... only half past four."

5 ".............. three miles to the station."

"Is it? .... too far to walk."

6 "Jean isn't coming to the party."

".............. a shame! She's so funny."

7 "This grey suit, sir? .... $350."

"Oh, dear. .... too expensive!"

8 ".............. a shame the Giants aren't playing."

"Yes, that would have been great."

12 請使用正確的 Wh 疑問詞或片語來完成問句。

1 "........................... wrapping paper is there?" "Three meters. It's enough for this big present."

2 "........................... emails are there in the in-box?" "Thirty. Dear me!"

3 "........................... is the new receptionist?" "Twenty-five. He's quite young."

4 "........................... are you late?" "Because I missed the bus."

5 "........................... is everybody?" "At the office Christmas party. Let's go too."

6 "........................... is your birthday?" "Tomorrow."

7 "........................... are you today?" "Fine, but still a bit tired."

8 "........................... is that over there?" "That's Chloe. She's my cousin."

9 "........................... is your car?" "The old blue one over there."

10 "........................... is your dad?" "Only about 1 m 60. He's quite short, really."

Reflecting on grammar

請研讀文法規則，再判斷以下說法是否正確。

		True	False
1	第三人稱單數動詞可搭配三種主格代名詞。		
2	第三人稱複數動詞可搭配三種主格代名詞。		
3	簡單現在式裡有三種 be 動詞。		
4	以 be 動詞為疑問句時，僅需改變說話的語調，不需改變語序。		
5	be 動詞的縮讀形式不常見於會話中。		
6	問句「Are you ready to go?」的答句是「Yes, I'm.」。		
7	文法上，必須依照一連串人事物裡的第一個名詞，來決定該使用 there is 或 there are。		
8	「There are a bottle of champagne and six glasses.」是正確的句子。		
9	Not there is 是 there is 的否定形式。		
10	Wh 疑問詞不一定要放在問句的句首。		

LESSON **1** 指示形容詞：this/that/these/those
Demonstratives: this/that/these/those

this 和 **that** 用於**單數名詞**；**these** 和 **those** 用於**複數名詞**。

this 和 these 用於指示**靠近講者**的人事物。 | that 和 those 用於指示和**講者有段距離**的人事物。

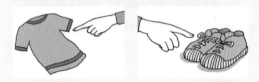

I like this T-shirt.　　I like these sneakers.

Do you like that hoodie?　　Do you like those jeans?

1 請參考圖片，使用合適的 this、that、these、those 等指示代名詞來完成對話。

Katie　Look at ⁰....these............ hats! They're great!

Tom　Yes, they're cool! And look at ¹........................ striped socks. I love them!

Katie　And what about ²........................ T-shirts here in the front? They're fantastic!

Tom　Mmm, yes. And ³........................ pants at the back are funny! I would definitely wear them!

Katie　They really go with ⁴........................ jacket over there.

Tom　Yes — what a great outfit!

Katie　The only thing I don't like much is ⁵........................ skirt near the pants.

Tom　No, it's a bit bright. Let's go in and buy something.

Katie　Yes! Cool!

---

❶ 指示形容詞後接名詞時，可具有形容詞的功能：
- **That** man is my uncle.
- **These** children are four years old.

❷ 指示形容詞還可作為**代名詞**：
- **This** is for you.
- **Those** are my friends.

❸ 指示形容詞的常見用途如下：

❶ 介紹某人：
- "**This** is my brother Steve." "Hello, Steve."

❷ 用來詢問某人是誰：
- "Who's **that**?" "It's Jim."

❸ 接電話時的自我介紹：
- **This** is Mrs. Jones speaking.

Q: 什麼時候要用 **this one** 或 **that one** 呢？

A: 代名詞 **one** 是用來取代一個**單數名詞**的。在兩項以上的物品裡做選擇時，需搭配 this 或 that 來表達完整句意，例如：「Which is your bag?」「This one.」。

Q: 是否也有代名詞 **ones** 的用法？

A: 有的，**ones** 用來取代一個**複數名詞**，並與 these 或 those 搭配使用。例如：「Which shoes do you prefer?」「These ones.」。

2 請使用 **this** 或 **that** 完成句子。

1 ....'s my new car over there.

2 Mr. Burnet, ... is Ms. Cooper, our new editor.

3 Which is your bag, this one or .... one over there?

4 Who's .... nice-looking boy near the door?

5 Good morning. .... is Howard Preston speaking.

6 "What's ....?"
"My new hat. Don't you like it?"

7 "............ is Carol. She's from England."
"Nice to meet you."

8 "Is .... you, Phil?" "Yes, it's me."

3 請重新排序單字來造句。

1 new / a / student / school / He's / this / in / .

....

2 good / is / This / news / !

....

3 are / These / cell phones / our / .

....

4 a / idea / That's / great / !

....

5 me / Give / magazines / please / those / . / ,

....

6 all / need/I / That's / .

....

7 is / This / my / friend / best / .

....

8 are / those / Who / two / guys / there / over / ?

....

4 請使用 **this**、**that**、**these** 或 **those** 來完成句子。

1 "Which apples would you like, madam?" "............ ones over there. The red ones."

2 "Who are .... children in the hall?" "They're Mr. Benson's children."

3 .... are Tom's school books. They aren't mine.

4 "Are you sure .... aren't your glasses?" "Of course. Look! I can't see anything with .... ones!"

5 "I really like .... T-shirt you're wearing." "............ one? It's really old!"

6 "Could you put .... flowers in .... vase over there, please?" "Yes, of course."

	複數可數名詞	不可數名詞
肯定句	There are **some** tomatoes.	There's **some** bread.
否定句	There aren't **any** tomatoes.	There isn't **any** bread.
疑問句	Are there **any** tomatoes?	Is there **any** bread?

❶ 提及特定數量或沒有限定數量的某物時，我們會在**肯定句**裡使用 **some**，在**否定**句和多數的**疑問句**裡使用 **any**。但這並非唯一準則，請參閱下方 FAQ。

❷ some 和 any 可作為形容詞，放在複數名詞或不可數名詞前面，亦可作為**代名詞**：

- "Are there any eggs? " "Yes, there are **some**."
- "Is there any sugar? " "No, there isn't **any**."

> ！ 我們會在單數可數名詞前面加上不定冠詞 a/an，看看下面的例子：
> - Have you got any brothers?（複數）
> - Have you got **a** brother?（單數）

1 請使用 a、an、some 或 any 來完成句子。

1 "Is there .... butter in the fridge?" "No, there isn't ...."

2 Here's .... money to pay the bills.

3 There isn't .... match today, but there's one tomorrow.

4 We have .... good friends in the USA.

5 "Have you got .... street map?" "Yes, here you are."

6 I don't have .... English dictionary.

7 Are there .... exams at the end of the school year?

8 We need to buy .... bread for dinner.

2 請使用下表的字詞，在筆記本寫下六個句子。

There's	a	important meeting	just around the corner.
		good news	on this island.
	an	fruit	in the kitchen.
		post office	this morning.
There are	some	children	in today's paper.
		fantastic beaches	in the playground.

FAQ

Q: 為什麼「Would you like some tea?」是用 some？問句不是應該使用 any 嗎？

A: 事實上，**主動示意、提出要求**，還有**預計會得到肯定**答覆的問句，一樣會使用 **some**，而 **any** 是用在詢問資訊的問句。請比較以下例句：

- Can I have **some** milk? → 意指「問有沒有牛奶可以喝，並預期答覆為**有**」
- Do we have **any** milk? → 意指「想知道還有沒有牛奶可以喝，**不確定**會聽到什麼答覆」

3 請先觀察 **A** 與 **B** 的簡短對話，並使用 some 或 any 來完成問句。接著請判斷如果是主動示意的問句，請寫 **O**；是提出要求的問句，請寫 **R**；是詢問資訊的問句，請寫 **I**。

1 A Can I have .... milk with my coffee?   **B** Yes, sure. ....

2 A Would you like .... sugar in your tea?   **B** No, thanks. ....

3 A Can you get me .... oranges from the supermarket?   **B** Okay. How many? ....

4 A Are there .... good shops in this street?   **B** I don't know really. ....

5 A Have you got .... new friends on Facebook?   **B** Yes, a lot! ....

6 A Do you want .... more juice?   **B** Yes, please. ....

UNIT
3
形容詞

! 請看以下例句：

• There is**n't any** cheese. → There**'s no** cheese.
• There are**n't any** tomatoes. → There **are no** tomatoes.

這兩句均有否定意義，但含**否定動詞**的句子需使用 **any**，含**肯定動詞**的句子則使用 **no**。
除了 no + 名詞，也可以使用代名詞 **none**：

• "Is there any flour?" "No, there's **no flour**." → No, there's **none**.
• "Are there any carrots?" "No, there are **no carrots**." → No, there are **none**.

FAQ

Q: 我有聽過「There isn't any rice left. Let's buy some.」，這裡的 left 是什麼意思？

A: left 是動詞 leave 的過去分詞，指「剩下的」；這句話的意思是「已經沒有米了」、「一粒米都不剩了」。

此意義的 left 亦可用於肯定句，如「There's some left.」，或是問句「Is there any left?」。

---

4 請使用 any、no 或 none 完成句子。

1 Are there .... questions? No? Let's go on, then.

2 There's .... more time. Hand in your papers now, please.

3 Sorry, there isn't .... ice cream left.

4 "Can I have some lemonade?" "Sorry, there's .... left. We finished it yesterday."

5 There's .... cheese in this sandwich. I don't like it without cheese.

6 "Have we got .... eggs?" "Let me see. No, we've got .... left, I'm afraid."

7 So there are .... tweets from the President Trump today. That's strange!

8 "How many 'likes' does your video have?" "It doesn't have .... so far."

FAQ

Q: 我有看過 any 用於肯定句的情況。為什麼會有這種用法？

A: 以肯定句來說，any 具有「**都可以**」、「**幾乎都是**」或「**沒有特別指定**」的意思：

• Come **any** time.（意指什麼時候來都可以）。
• "Which sandwich would you like?" "**Any**. I don't mind."
（意指幾乎所有三明治都可以，沒有偏好哪一種口味。）

> 如果覺得不太容易記住 some、any 和 no 的使用時機，可以試試這個方法。
> 想像一下原子裡面的粒子，也就是質子、中子和電子。some 具有**肯定**意義，就像**質子**帶有正電荷；**any** 不具肯定意義，也不具否定意義，就和**中子**一樣；no 具有**否定**意義，如同帶負電荷的**電子**。

5 請以 some 或 any 來完成以下對話。

1 A Mom, can I go out tonight?
   B Yes, okay, but you mustn't come back late.
   A Don't worry. I'll be home by ten. Er . . . and can I have [1].............. money?
   B Well, I haven't got [2].............. cash, but you can ask Dad.

2 A Is there [1].............. fruit left? I want to make [2].............. fruit salad.
   B Yes, there are [3].............. apples, [4].............. peaches and [5].............. grapes, but there aren't [6].............. pears.
   A Never mind. [7].............. kind of fruit will do.

3 A What kind of novels do you like reading?
   B [1].............. type — adventure, love stories, thrillers. . . . I love all kinds of novels.

4 A There isn't [1].............. paper in the printer. Can you get [2]..............? It's in the drawer on the left.
   B Ah, yes, here you are. Is there [3].............. ink in the cartridge?
   A Yes, there's still [4].............. left.

LESSON 3 性狀形容詞／國籍形容詞／形容詞在句中位置的順序
Qualifying adjectives and adjectives of nationality; order of adjectives

性狀形容詞

	單數	複數
陽性	a **shy** boy	some **shy** boys
陰性	a **shy** girl	some **shy** girls
中性	an **interesting** museum	some **interesting** museums

1 性狀形容詞用來描述人事物的性格或狀態，此類形容詞永遠不會從單數變為複數，或從陽性變為陰性。放在句中修飾名詞的性狀時，一定要放在名詞**前面**，不能放在後面：

• It's a **modern** <u>apartment</u>.　• I don't like **arrogant** <u>people</u>.

2 但如果性狀形容詞是用於描述動作或狀態，可放在 **be 動詞**、**get**、**look**、**seem**、**feel** 等其他感官動詞的**後面**：

• I'm **tired**.　• I <u>feel</u> **great**.　• Sally <u>looks</u> **sad**.　• It's <u>getting</u> **dark**.

Focus

請看下方兩個例句，在 be 動詞問句裡，形容詞作為述部（即描述主角的動作或狀態的部分）時，會放在主詞後面：

• Is <u>Jennifer</u> **Irish**?　• Are <u>the students</u> **worried** about the exam?

1 請將句中的形容詞畫上**底線**，然後重新排序單字，在筆記本上寫出邏輯通順的句子。

1 a / day / hot / today / it's / .
2 is / there / my / village / small / church / a/in / .
3 these / comfortable / are / chairs / ?
4 looks / the / house / big / square / abandoned / the / in / .
5 are / children / in / there / some / young / park / the / .
6 tower / view / the / is / from / fantastic / the / .
7 famous / expensive / restaurant / this/is / ?
8 is / a / clothes shop / new/there / the / on / street / main/.

2 下方部分句子有誤，請找出錯誤並訂正。

1 There are two bigs computer labs in our school. ....
2 Is ready your brother for his final exam? ....
3 Fatima is a good student. ....
4 The school building looks big, but there are only 20 classrooms. ....
5 Are happy your parents with your school results? ....
6 Mr. Ross always gives speeches interesting. ....
7 Some youngs boys are playing in the park. ....
8 This is an amusing TV series. ....

國籍形容詞

除了某些特例情況外，國籍形容詞是以相關的國家或洲別名稱，加上**字尾**所組成。
以下列出最為常見的**字尾**。

–an/–ian		–ish		–ese		不規則變化	
Italy	Italian	Sweden	Swedish	China	Chinese	France	French
Germany	German	Britain	British	Portugal	Portuguese	Greece	Greek
Canada	Canadian	Denmark	Danish	Japan	Japanese	Netherlands	Dutch
Europe	European	Scotland	Scottish	Senegal	Senegalese	Switzerland	Swiss
Australia	Australian	England	English	Congo	Congolese	Wales	Welsh
Brazil	Brazilian	Turkey	Turkish	Sudan	Sudanese	Pakistan	Pakistani

1 書寫國籍形容詞時，**首字母**一定要**大寫**。若國籍形容詞**未加冠詞**，通常會變成**名詞**，指該國的**語言**：
   • I love **English**.   • I don't speak **French**.
2 在國籍代名詞前面加上 **the**，則代表該國的**人民**：
   • **The** <u>Dutch</u> speak English as a second language.

形容詞的順序

當一個名詞需搭配兩個以上的形容詞時，表達**看法**的形容詞通常會放在偏**敘述性**的形容詞**前面**。
下表依序列出最常見的形容詞排列順序：

不定冠詞／數量形容詞／所有格形容詞	看法	尺寸	年齡	形狀	顏色	國籍	材質
a some my your	lovely nice expensive famous	small large huge tall	new ancient old young	round square circular	white red blue green	Chinese African American	cotton gold silver wood

• She's <u>a</u> <u>famous</u> <u>Italian</u> writer.
• Do you like <u>my</u> <u>ancient</u> <u>Chinese</u> pearl earrings?
• I bought <u>two</u> <u>lovely</u> <u>small</u> <u>rectangular</u> <u>Persian</u> rugs.

3 請運用提示用詞，來大致描述以下每件骨董店的商品。

0 silver / small / teapot / antique
A small, antique, silver teapot..........

1 porcelain / fruit bowl / Chinese / blue and white

2 painting / abstract / oil / large

3 wooden / neoclassical / French / chest of drawers

4 old / five / Italian / silver / coffee spoons

5 paperweight / Venetian / white and violet / glass

4 請正確排序形容詞來完成句子。

1 The girls are wearing .... jackets. (leather / American / black / expensive)

2 Here's a .... elephant for your collection. (ebony / valuable / African / old)

3 Why don't you buy that .... dress? (simple / cotton / green)

4 Let's sit around this .... table. (plastic / dark green / oval)

5 The new teacher is a .... man. Everyone likes him!
(young / Canadian / tall / handsome)

6 His girlfriend has got .... hair. (blonde / long / straight)

7 There's a .... spider in my bedroom. (black / big / horrible)

LESSON 4 數字和日期 Numbers and dates

基數

❶ 除了 one 之外，所有數字的後面均需加上**複數名詞**：
- five children
- seven days
- four seasons
- ten dollars
- 12 months

❷ 13 到 19 之間的數字，字尾是 **teen**，如 thir<u>teen</u>、four<u>teen</u> 等

❸ 以 10 為倍數的數字，字尾是 **ty**，如 twen<u>ty</u>、thir<u>ty</u> 等

❹ 百位數後面要加 **and**，來連接後面的十位數與個位數，如：
168 → one hundred <u>and</u> sixty-eight
2,340 → two thousand three hundred <u>and</u> forty

FAQ

Q: 我知道 teenager 是指 13 歲到 19 歲的年輕人，因為這些數字的字尾都有 **teen**，但我也聽過有人說 **tweenagers**，這是指哪個年齡層的人呢？

A: tweenagers 或 tweens 源自 between，代表 10 到 12 歲的人，因為這個年齡層的人剛好介於（between）兒童期與青春期。

1 請將金額的阿拉伯數字與念法配對。

.... **1** $223.50   **A** eighty one dollars and thirty cents

.... **2** $243.15   **B** two hundred forty-three dollars and fifteen cents

.... **3** $44   **C** sixty-five dollars

.... **4** $65   **D** eighteen dollars and forty cents

.... **5** $81.30   **E** forty-four dollars

.... **6** $18.40   **F** two hundred twenty-three dollars and fifty cents

Focus

❶ 英文會以**逗號**隔開每一個**千進位數字**，並以**句號**分隔**小數和整數**。小數必須**逐一唸出**：

10,000 = ten thousand │ 3.14 = three point one four │ 25.46 = twenty five point four six

100 = a hundred / one hundred │ 1,000 = a thousand / one thousand

1,000,000 = a million / one million │ 1,000,000,000 = a billion / one billion

❷ 放在數字後面的 hundred、thousand、million 和 billion 不需要加 s 變成複數，只有在具有「**若干**」、「**未指定數量**」的意思時，才需要**加 s**。在此情況下，此類單字後方必須依序加上 **of** 與名詞：

- six <u>hundred</u> meters `BUT` <u>hundred**s**</u> of meters（上百公尺）
- four <u>thousand</u> people `BUT` <u>thousand**s**</u> of people（上千人）

UNIT 3 形容詞

2 請圈出正確的用字。

1 Shhh . . . I'm counting! . . . **two hundred twenty-five / two hundred and twenty-five**.

2 This precious watch cost several **hundreds / hundred** of dollars.

3 Nearly five **thousands / thousand** people were at the concert last night.

4 **Thousands / Thousand** of people were cheering the rock star.

5 About four **millions / million** people watched the *Master Chef USA* final last Saturday.

6 This jacket is really expensive. Look: **two and hundred five pounds / two hundred and five pounds**.

7 There are eight **hundreds thirty-three / hundred and thirty-three** students in our school.

8 255 divided by a hundred is **two point fifty-five / two point five five**.

9 **Thousand / Thousands** of people died in the tsunami.

10 **Two thousands and seven / Two thousand and seven** people ran in the half-marathon last month.

序數詞

❶ 多數序數詞的結構為**基數 + th**：

four → four**th** │ six → six**th** │ ten → ten**th** │ eleven → eleven**th**

❷ 但請注意 one → **first**、two → **second**、three → **third**，因此像 twenty-first、twenty-second、twenty-third 或 thirty-first 等會沿用此表達方式。

❸ 序數詞亦可採用縮寫的書寫形式，例如：10th、21st、22nd、23rd 等。

❹ 請留意以下序數詞的拼法：

five → **fifth** │ eight → eigh**th** │ nine → nin**th** │ twelve → twel**fth** │
twenty → twent**ieth** │ thirty → thirt**ieth** │ forty → fort**ieth**
（所有十的倍數拼字方式均以此類推）

❺ 序數詞前面要加定冠詞 **the**：

the second prize │ Queen Elizabeth I (the first) │ King Henry VIII (the eighth)

FAQ

Q: 英文的分數要怎麼唸呢？

A: **分子**需以**基數**表達，**分母**則需以單數或複數的**序數詞**表達：

1/4：one fourth/quarter │ 2/3：two-thirds
3/5：three-fifths │ `BUT` 1/2：one half

3 請拼出序數詞。

1 Yesterday was our 20th (..........................) wedding anniversary.

2 My hotel room is on the 5th (...................) floor.

3 What was life like in the 13th (................................) century?

4 When's your 16th (...................................) birthday?

5 This cathedral dates back to the 12th (..............................) century.

6 He came 2nd (...........................) in the race. It was his best time ever.

7 Alaska is the 49th (........................) state of the USA and Hawaii is the 50th (........................).

日期

我們用**縮寫序數詞**的方式來表達**日期**：

• July 7th (the seventh of July)　　• May 31st (the thirty-first of May)

FAQ

Q: 我收到一封從英國寄來的信，信上日期寫「03/06/2020」，意思是 6 月 3 日，不是 3 月 6 日。真的很難判斷……。

A: **英式**英文會先表達**日期**，再表達**月分**，例如 7 月 9 日寫成 09/07、5 月 31 日寫成 31/05。很重要，這一定要記住！

年分

年分的表達方式如下：

• **1565** → fifteen sixty-five　　• **1992** → nineteen ninety-two
• **2018** → twenty eighteen / two thousand and eighteen

但要注意：

• **221 B.C.** → two hundred and twenty-one B.C.（B.C. = before Christ 西元前）
• **210 A.D.** → two hundred and ten A.D.（A.D. = Anno Domini = after Christ 西元後）
• **1600** → sixteen hundred　　• **1605** → sixteen hundred and five / sixteen oh-five
• in the twenties of the 20th century（以「十年」為一個單位的表達方式）

4 請寫出日期的縮寫。美式寫法的後面請加（**Am.E.**），英式寫法的後面請加（**Br.E.**）。

1 June the ninth, twenty sixteen
June 9th, 2016 (Am.E.)
....

2 The first of January, two thousand
....

3 The twenty-third of April, two thousand and five
....

4 March the seventeenth, nineteen sixty-nine
....

5 July the fourth, Independence Day
....

6 The ninth of November, two thousand and eleven
....

7 The thirtieth of January, twenty fourteen
....

8 January the first, New Year's Day
....

5 請以阿拉伯數字寫出分數。

1 two-ninths = ...
2 four-sevenths = ...
3 four-fifteenths = ...
4 seven-eighteenths = ...

5 five-eighths = ...
6 three-fifths = ...
7 six-seventeenths = ...
8 two-elevenths = ...

Focus

阿拉伯數字 0 有不同的英文書寫方式：

1 表示溫度，我們說 zero：
- It's quite cold today. It's ten degrees below **zero**.

−10°

2 表示數學的零，我們說 zero 或 nought（英式英文）：
- 0.58 → **zero** point five eight

3 表示電話號碼，我們說 zero 或 oh：
- Susan's phone number is 171 3400518 （one seven one, three four double **oh** five one eight）

4 表示運動賽事的分數，我們通常說 nil：
- Leicester has just won three goals to **nil**.

5 表示網球比賽的分數，我們說 love：
- The score in this game is thirty **love**.

Thirty love!

---

6 請針對下方情況，寫出 **0** 的正確說法。

1 In Helsinki it is -12°C.

In Helsinki it is twelve degrees below ....

2 It's 40−0 to Murray.

It's forty .... to Murray.

3 It's 2−0 to Chelsea.

It's two .... to Chelsea.

4 James Bond is a 00 agent.

James Bond is a double .... agent.

5 He got 0/10 on the test.

He got .... out of ten on the test.

6 The first answer on the quiz is 0.21.

The first answer on the quiz is .... point two one.

7 Our room number is 202.

Our room number is two .... two .

8 The diameter of the hole is 0.65 cm.

The diameter of the hole is .... point six five centimeters.

9 My phone number is 07793 294546.

My phone number is .... double seven nine three, two nine four five four six.

請學習以下數字和百分比的說法：
- **Four out of five** of the boys in the class like playing football.
- **Twenty-five percent** of the kids go to school by car.
- Jimmy scored **ten out of ten** in the test; he got all the answers right.
- This week there's **twenty percent** discount on electrical appliances in the local supermarket.

ROUND UP 3

1 請改寫為複數句子。

1 This is my friend. ....

2 That is his dog. ....

3 This is our sister. ....

4 That is your student. ....

5 That is their car. ....

2 請使用 some 或 any 完成句子。

1 I haven't got .... money with me. Could you lend me .... ?

2 There's .... interesting information on this website.

3 Have you got .... news from the German school?

4 .... students are working on a project about the history of the EU.

5 Our school hasn't got .... Erasmus partners in Italy.

6 "Are there .... teachers in the staff room?" "No, they're all in their classrooms."

7 "Have you got .... blue pens?" "Yes, we have .... in this box."

8 The children don't have .... computers in their class.

9 We live in a very small town. There aren't .... hotels, but there are .... lively pubs.

10 There isn't .... housework to do today.

延伸補充

❶ none of us 在我們這群人裡面，沒有一個人⋯⋯
none of you 在你們這群人裡面，沒有一個人⋯⋯
none of them 在這群人事物裡，沒有一個人事物⋯⋯
none of these 這些東西裡，沒有一個東西⋯⋯
none of those 那些東西裡，沒有一個東西⋯⋯
none of my friends 我的朋友裡，沒有一個人⋯⋯

❷ 「none of . . .」的用法後面可接**單數動詞**或**複數動詞**：
- **None of these people** <u>works/work</u> in a factory.
- **None of us** <u>is/are</u> going to the movies tonight.

---

3 請使用 no 或 none 完成句子。

1 "Can I have a French magazine, please?" "Sorry, there are .... left."

2 We were lucky. We found .... difficulties in carrying out this project.

3 Great! There are .... lessons tomorrow.

4 .... of them arrived in time.

5 There are .... good restaurants in this little town.

6 .... sensible person would behave like that.

7 .... of the local museums are open today. It's a national holiday.

8 "Did any students hand in their reports yesterday?" "No, sorry. ...."

延伸補充

some、any 和 no 亦具有以下特殊用法：

❶ some + 單數可數名詞時，意思是「某程度的」、「非特定的」意義：
- They live in **some** <u>village</u> in this valley.

❷ 放在數字前面的 **some**，意指「大約」、「或多或少」：
- The nearest hospital is **some** <u>30</u> km from here.

❸ any 和 **no** 是放在比較級和形容詞 **good** 前面的副詞，後面可接**動詞 ing**：
- Is it **any** <u>better</u> after a hot cup of tea?
- Was it **any** <u>good talking</u> to your principal?

❹ no + 形容詞 + 名詞意指「完全不是」、「絲毫沒有」：
- I'm **no** <u>great singer</u>.

❺ no 亦可用於表達禁令：
- **No** smoking in the school premises.

---

4 請在句中有誤處畫底線，並訂正為正確的句子。

1 No shops aren't open today. It's a holiday.

....

2 I haven't no homework to do for tomorrow.

....

3 "Are there any restaurants in this street?" "No, there aren't none."

....

4 Not any patients are allowed in this area.

....

5 None journalists can get into the room.

....

6 It's no any use crying over spilt milk.

....

7 The airport must be any 20 miles from here.

....

8 We're some good at painting. We're really hopeless!

....

---

5 請使用正確的名詞或形容詞來完成句子。

1 My friend Sintija lives in Helsinki, but she isn't .... She was born in Latvia from .... parents.

2 Montreal is a cosmopolitan .... city where people speak English and French.

3 There's a .... girl in my class. She arrived from Thailand two months ago.

4 Helen is in Germany because she wants to improve her .... She needs it for her job.

5 Brussels is the capital city of .... and the seat of the Council of ....

6 Van Basten comes from .... He's Dutch.

6 請選出正確的答案。

1 .... are allowed in these rooms.

Ⓐ None visitors   Ⓑ No visitors   Ⓒ No visitor

2 "Is there any tea in the teapot?" "No, ..."

Ⓐ there's none   Ⓑ there's some   Ⓒ there's no

3 .... museums are open in town today because it's Monday.

Ⓐ Not any   Ⓑ None   Ⓒ No

4 I don't have .... homework for tomorrow.

Ⓐ any   Ⓑ no   Ⓒ some

5 I need a .... table for my garden.

Ⓐ new square plastic   Ⓑ plastic new square   Ⓒ square plastic new

6 "........." "No, I think he's Spanish."

Ⓐ Is Scottish the new receptionist?   Ⓑ Is the new Scottish receptionist?

Ⓒ Is the new receptionist Scottish?

7 Steve was born on January ....

Ⓐ 12nd   Ⓑ 12th   Ⓒ 12rd

8 Joanne lives on the .... floor.

Ⓐ fiveth   Ⓑ fifeth   Ⓒ fifth

9 .... of cell phone buyers are under 18.

Ⓐ One third   Ⓑ One threeth   Ⓒ One threerd

10 The company invested two .... dollars to renovate its old factories.

Ⓐ billions   Ⓑ billion   Ⓒ milliards

11 It's really cold tonight. It's five degrees below ....

Ⓐ nought   Ⓑ nil   Ⓒ zero

12 Chelsea FC is winning three goals to ....

Ⓐ nil   Ⓑ nought   Ⓒ love

13 .... my family lives in the United States.

Ⓐ A half   Ⓑ Half   Ⓒ The half

14 Nadal is leading in the final set by three games to ....

Ⓐ zero   Ⓑ nil   Ⓒ love

基本的數學四則運算   延伸補充

❶ 加法

$5 + 8 = 13$ → five **plus** eight equals thirteen / five **and** eight is thirteen

❷ 減法

$12 - 4 = 8$ → twelve **minus** four equals eight / four **from** twelve is eight

❸ 乘法

$4 \times 5 = 20$ → four **multiplied by** five equals twenty / four **times** five is twenty

❹ 除法

$32 \div 4 = 8$ → thirty-two **divided by** four equals eight / four **into** thirty-two is eight

更複雜的數學運算

1 指數和指數函數

底數 (base) $\longrightarrow$ 3^2 $\longleftarrow$ 指數 (exponent)

- $b^x = y$ → b **(raised) to the** xth **power equals y**（b 的 x 次方等於 y）
- $4^2 = 16$ → four **squared** equals sixteen / four **(raised) to the second power** equals sixteen
  （4 的平方等於 16／4 的二次方等於 16）
- $7^3 = 343$ → seven **cubed** equals three hundred and forty-three /
  seven **(raised) to the third power** equals three hundred and forty-three
  （7 的立方等於 343／7 的三次方等於 343）

2 根號

指數 (index) $\longrightarrow$
根號 (radical symbol) $\longrightarrow$ $\sqrt[3]{64}$ $\longleftarrow$ 根號的自變數 (argument of the radical/radicand)

$\sqrt{16} = 4$ → **the square root of** sixteen equals four（16 開平方根等於 4）

$\sqrt[3]{90} \fallingdotseq 4.48$ → **the cubic root of** ninety is approximately four point four eight
（90 開立方根約等於 4.48）

3 對數和對數函數

$$\log_6 (216) = 3$$

底數(base) $\nearrow$　自變數 (argument)

- $\log_b (y) = x$ → **logarithm base** b **of** y equals x（以 b 為底數時，y 的對數等於 x）
- $\log_2 (8) = 3$ → **logarithm base** two **of** eight equals three（以 2 為底數時，8 的對數等於 3）

Reflecting on grammar

請研讀文法規則，再判斷以下說法是否正確。

		True	False
1	that 的複數形式是 these。		
2	想主動示意或要求某事而提問時，需使用 some 而不是 any。		
3	any 不能用於肯定句。		
4	no 需要搭配否定動詞。		
5	「None of us are ready.」是錯誤的句子。		
6	在形容詞作為述部的 be 動詞問句中，形容詞會放在名詞的前面。		
7	國籍形容詞的首字母一定是小寫。		
8	「Have you seen the amazing new French science-fiction movie?」此句子的形容詞排序正確。		
9	我收到的信上日期是寫 03.21.2016，所以可能是來自美國的信。		
10	所有序數詞均以基數加上 th 所構成。		

Revision and Exams 1 (UNITS 1 – 2 – 3)

1 請以 **a、an** 或 **the** 來完成下方的電子郵件，並在不需要冠詞的部位，寫上「///」符號。

From: **Asta** astalas@gmail.com
To: **Julie** julieb99@yahoo.com

Hi Julie!

I'm Asta, your new key pal. My teacher gave me your email address. She says we can do an e-twinning project this year.

I'm 16. I'm Lithuanian and I live in Vilnius, [1].............. capital city of [2].............. Lithuania. Do you know where [3].............. my country is? It's in [4].............. north-east of Europe, near [5].............. Russia and [6].............. Poland. It isn't big, but it's [7].............. interesting country on [8].............. Baltic Sea.

I'm [9].............. student at secondary school and I study [10].............. English. I like [11].............. languages and I like traveling.

Tell me about yourself and send me [12].............. photo. You'll find [13].............. photo of [14].............. my city cathedral in [15].............. attachment.

Write soon,
Asta

2 請使用正確的 **be** 動詞形式來完成短文。

Things [1].............. different in my family these days. I [2].............. a member of a big family now and I [3].............. an only child any more. My dad and Maria [4].............. married now, so she [5].............. my new stepmother. And there [6].............. three children in Maria's family: Ann, Emma and Luke. We all live together in their big house in the country. We have a lot of fun and we [7].............. all good friends. I think it [8].............. great being part of a big family!

3 請使用下方單字來完成短文。注意必須採用複數名詞，且動詞要有三態變化。

| ox | sheep | cow | be (x3) |
| duck | goose | deer | bush |

In the first scene of the movie, two [1]........................... are pulling a cart along a country path. It all seems peaceful and quiet, but the scene changes and you see a field with some [2]........................... and [3]........................... standing still in an unnatural silence. In the pond of a farm nearby, there [4]........................... some [5]........................... and [6]..........................., but they are not moving — they're just floating on the water, absolutely still, as if they were frozen. Two [7]........................... with big antlers are hiding behind some [8]........................... and they are not moving either. There [9]........................... a gloomy atmosphere, as if something terrible were going to happen. [10]........................... you curious to see what happens? Go and see the movie this weekend. It's quite scary!

4 選出正確的答案。

I like living in ¹...... little town. ²...... everything I need and everything I like doing. I'm ³...... journalist and all I need for my work is ⁴...... computer and ⁵...... Internet connection. Here all the houses have broadband, so I can easily work from home.

⁶...... a railway station with lots of trains to and from London from early morning to late in the evening. About ⁷...... of the inhabitants work or study in London.

I like to take some exercise in my free time. There ⁸...... some gyms and a sports center in town, but there isn't ⁹...... indoor swimming pool. There's a theater too. Every winter, there's a drama festival that goes on for over two weeks. ¹⁰...... of the performances are really good and attract lots of people from nearby places.

In the evenings, I usually go to my favorite pub on the High Street. ¹¹...... of the other pubs have the same kind of "vintage" atmosphere as The Crown and Anchor. The landlord is a good friend of mine and ¹²...... of the patrons are too. We really enjoy spending time together.

1	Ⓐ that	Ⓑ this	Ⓒ any
2	Ⓐ There are	Ⓑ There isn't	Ⓒ There's
3	Ⓐ //	Ⓑ the	Ⓒ a
4	Ⓐ the	Ⓑ some	Ⓒ a
5	Ⓐ an	Ⓑ a	Ⓒ //
6	Ⓐ There are	Ⓑ There's	Ⓒ There isn't
7	Ⓐ three-fourth	Ⓑ three-fours	Ⓒ three-quarters
8	Ⓐ aren't	Ⓑ are	Ⓒ is
9	Ⓐ any	Ⓑ an	Ⓒ a
10	Ⓐ Some	Ⓑ No	Ⓒ Every
11	Ⓐ None	Ⓑ No	Ⓒ Some
12	Ⓐ some	Ⓑ none	Ⓒ any

5 請將括號裡的形容詞正確排序，並依序填空，來完成珍娜特（Janet）寫給朋友艾琳（Irene）的電子郵件。

Hi Irene,

I've been surfing the net and I've just seen some ¹... clothes on sale on a ²........................... website. (popular, trendy, great)

There are ³.. jackets that cost only $20.00. They are ⁴..........................., aren't they? (cheap, eco-leather, colorful)

And the T-shirts! ⁵........................... , ... or .... , ...

T-shirts at the ⁶........................... price of $1 — yes, one dollar! — each. (cotton, white, black, incredible, long-sleeved)

I wanted to buy a really ⁷... miniskirt, but my mom said no. (denim, short, tight)

But she let me buy a ⁸... dress. It's ⁹........................... for the summer! (fantastic, blue, low-necked, long) I'm sending you the link to the website. There's a ¹⁰... dress that you'll love. (evening, glittery, long)

Let me know.

Janet

6 請使用正確的 be 動詞或 have 來完成短文。

Welcome to Snowdonia
National Park

Snowdonia National Park [1]..................... vast areas of natural beauty and unique scenery. Its Welsh name can [2].................... translated as "the place of the eagles."

The park, which covers 838 square miles, [3]..................... one of the three natural parks found in Wales and the oldest one, being designated as one in 1951. The area of the Snowdonia National Park [4]..................... so much to offer to visitors that if you are visiting it for the first time, you will wonder why it took you so long to do it.

The landscape [5]..................... breathtaking and unique. There [6]..................... nine mountain ranges here and they cover over half of the national park's surface. Some of the peaks [7]..................... over 3,000 feet (915 m).

Snowdonia offers first-class accommodation in a number of hotels and bed and breakfasts.

FOR MORE INFORMATION, PLEASE PHONE 01766 770274 OR SEND AN EMAIL TO park@snowdonia-npa.gov.uk.

7 請以最貼切的單字完成本篇克漏字。每一格僅能填入一個單字。

The British Isles

The British Isles [1]..................... an archipelago in [2]..................... north-west of Europe. Great Britain is [3]..................... biggest island. It [4]..................... surrounded by the English Channel, [5]..................... North Sea, the Irish Sea and the Atlantic Ocean. Ireland is [6]..................... other big island of the archipelago. Northern Ireland belongs to the United Kingdom, like England, Scotland and Wales. [7]..................... rest of the island is [8]..................... independent country, called the Republic of Ireland. [9]..................... Pennines are the backbone of England, while the Thames [10]..................... the most important river, which flows through [11]..................... country from west to east. The Shannon is the longest river in Ireland. The biggest lake in Scotland [12]..................... Loch Lomond, but the most famous is Loch Ness because of Nessie, the monster which is said to live in its dark deep water.

8 請閱讀以下短文，選出最符合的答案。

My brother is self-sufficient. He doesn't have ⁰ a ...... job and lives in ¹...... cottage in the country where he grows all his own vegetables. In spring, there are ²...... lettuces in his garden, but there aren't ³...... tomatoes. In summer, there ⁴...... tomatoes, but ⁵...... lettuces. He also has ⁶...... fruit trees with cherries and plums, but ⁷...... apple trees. There ⁸...... any cherries at the moment, but there are ⁹...... plums. He always gives me ¹⁰...... when I visit him.

	Ⓐ		Ⓑ		Ⓒ		Ⓓ	
0	Ⓐ the		Ⓑ an		Ⓒ a		Ⓓ /	
1	Ⓐ an		Ⓑ a		Ⓒ /		Ⓓ the	
2	Ⓐ none		Ⓑ some		Ⓒ the		Ⓓ any	
3	Ⓐ no		Ⓑ any		Ⓒ none		Ⓓ some	
4	Ⓐ are		Ⓑ haven't		Ⓒ isn't		Ⓓ aren't	
5	Ⓐ no		Ⓑ any		Ⓒ some		Ⓓ none	
6	Ⓐ any		Ⓑ the		Ⓒ none		Ⓓ some	
7	Ⓐ some		Ⓑ no		Ⓒ any		Ⓓ none	
8	Ⓐ are		Ⓑ have		Ⓒ aren't		Ⓓ haven't	
9	Ⓐ some		Ⓑ no		Ⓒ any		Ⓓ none	
10	Ⓐ any		Ⓑ no		Ⓒ none		Ⓓ some	

9 根據前後文，填入最貼切的單字。每一格僅能填入一個單字。可參考第 **0** 格的示範。

English, an international language

English is spoken in many parts of ⁰ ...... the ...... world and is the official language in various International institutions, like ¹............ United Nations. ²............ is also considered the language of science, commerce and technology and it is used in international aviation and navigation.

Here are the countries where English is spoken today:

³............ people speak it as their mother tongue, for example, in ⁴............ USA, Britain, Ireland, Australia, New Zealand, most of Canada and ⁵............ of the Caribbean countries.

Some people speak it as ⁶............ official language; this means that nearly everybody understands it and ⁷............ speak it in government offices, the media and education. Examples of this are India, Singapore, Kenya and South Africa.

And a lot more people speak it as ⁸............ foreign language, because they learn it at school or at university.

But why is English so important? One reason is historical. Great Britain was the center of an enormous empire in ⁹............ 19th century, and English was the language of her colonies all over the world. Another reason is linked to the economic and cultural prestige that the United States acquired in ¹⁰............ 20th century — and still has today — in the field of science and technology.

Towards Competences

你將參加交換學生活動，與某澳洲學校交流。老師要求你撰寫一篇短文，向寄宿家庭自我介紹。下表是老師給你的資料。完成下表，聊聊你喜歡與不喜歡的事情、你的嗜好，以及有需要特別注意的過敏症或請求。

Australia 🇦🇺 **School Exchange**

Presentation for your host family

_____

_____

_____

_____

_____

Sign here _____

> Stick your photo here.

Self Check 1

請選出答案，再至解答頁核對正確與否。

1 There are still some .... on that tree.
  Ⓐ leafs Ⓑ leaves Ⓒ leavs

2 The .... are standing near the jewelry store.
  Ⓐ policewomens Ⓑ policewoman Ⓒ policewomen

3 Where .... the scissors?
  Ⓐ is Ⓑ are Ⓒ aren't

4 Listen! This is an interesting ....
  Ⓐ news Ⓑ piece of news Ⓒ new

5 The crossroads near our office .... very dangerous. Lots of accidents happen there.
  Ⓐ aren't Ⓑ is Ⓒ isn't

6 The latest .... are very reliable.
  Ⓐ analyses Ⓑ analysis Ⓒ analysises

7 Oh no! There are dog .... on the sofa again. Why can't he sleep in his basket?
  Ⓐ hair Ⓑ hairs Ⓒ haires

8 My wife ....
  Ⓐ does the nurse Ⓑ is the nurse Ⓒ is a nurse

9 I haven't got .... umbrella with me.
  Ⓐ an Ⓑ the Ⓒ a

10 Jeff plays .... violin very well.
  Ⓐ // Ⓑ a Ⓒ the

11 .... breakfast is served on the terrace.
  Ⓐ The Ⓑ A Ⓒ //

12 Spain is in .... south-west of Europe.
  Ⓐ the Ⓑ // Ⓒ a

13 Paul and I are good friends. .... work in the same office.
  Ⓐ You Ⓑ They Ⓒ We

14 .... ten dollars fifty.
  Ⓐ There's Ⓑ It's Ⓒ Is

15 Jane .... from England. She's Australian, from Melbourne.
  Ⓐ is Ⓑ aren't Ⓒ isn't

16 Can I have a glass of water, please? I'm really ....
  Ⓐ hungry Ⓑ hurry Ⓒ thirsty

17 Kirsty and I .... in a hurry because it's late.
  Ⓐ am Ⓑ are Ⓒ is

18 Strange! There .... any lights in this room.
  Ⓐ are Ⓑ aren't Ⓒ isn't

19 Your room is 203. .... your key.

Ⓐ Here   Ⓑ There is

Ⓒ Here is

20 There .... a new smartphone and a special watch in that shop window. Let's go in and ask how much they are.

Ⓐ are   Ⓑ aren't   Ⓒ is

21 .... "No, she's out."

Ⓐ "Is your sister there?"

Ⓑ "Is there your sister?"

Ⓒ "Is here your sister?"

22 .... is your favorite ice cream flavor? Chocolate or vanilla?

Ⓐ How   Ⓑ What   Ⓒ Which

23 "How .... is it from the station to your office?" "500 meters."

Ⓐ long   Ⓑ far   Ⓒ much

24 "How .... is that bridge?" "150 meters."

Ⓐ long   Ⓑ much   Ⓒ deep

25 "What's the hotel like?"

Ⓐ "It's small and cozy."

Ⓑ "I like it very much."

Ⓒ "I don't like it at all."

26 I like .... pants over there.

Ⓐ those   Ⓑ this   Ⓒ that

27 Is there .... street map of London?

Ⓐ some   Ⓑ a   Ⓒ any

28 Can I have .... salt, please?

Ⓐ some   Ⓑ a   Ⓒ any

29 There isn't .... ink left in the printer cartridge.

Ⓐ some   Ⓑ any   Ⓒ no

30 There are some .... in our town. There are concerts every week.

Ⓐ greats venues

Ⓑ venues greats

Ⓒ great venues

31 "Have you got .... relatives in China, Liu?" "Yes, I've got three cousins."

Ⓐ some   Ⓑ any   Ⓒ the

32 It's .... good playing squash twice a week and having two hamburgers after each match.

Ⓐ no   Ⓑ any   Ⓒ some

33 He studied at .... university in the south of the country.

Ⓐ no   Ⓑ some   Ⓒ any

34 .... with her new job?

Ⓐ Susan is she happy

Ⓑ Is happy Susan

Ⓒ Is Susan happy

35 Look at that lovely .... table by the window!

Ⓐ small, round, wooden

Ⓑ wooden, small, round

Ⓒ round, wooden, small

36 My daughter likes .... cats very much.

Ⓐ soft, white, Persian

Ⓑ Persian, white, soft

Ⓒ soft, Persian, white

37 There are .... people at the concert tonight.

Ⓐ seven hundreds and fifty

Ⓑ seven hundred fifty

Ⓒ seven hundred and fifty

38 Claire was born on March ....

Ⓐ 22rd   Ⓑ 22nd   Ⓒ 22th

39 The temperature today is five degrees below ....

Ⓐ nought   Ⓑ nil   Ⓒ zero

40 "What's the .... root of 25?" "It's five."

Ⓐ cubic   Ⓑ square   Ⓒ checked

Assess yourself!

☐ 0 - 10   還要多加用功。

☐ 11 - 20   尚可。

☐ 21 - 30   不錯。

☐ 31 - 40   非常好！

動詞 have 和所有格 Verb *have* and Possessives

LESSON 1 動詞 have：肯定句 Verb have — positive form　　**→ 圖解請見P. 405**

動詞 **have** 具有兩種形式：**have** 和 **has**（用於單數第三人稱）。英式英語通常會搭配 **got** 來強調句意，尤其使用縮讀形式。

完整形式	縮讀形式
I have got	I've got
you have got	you've got
he has got	he's got
she has got	she's got
it has got	it's got
we have got	we've got
you have got	you've got
they have got	they've got

◆ **切記！**

主詞是**名詞**時，亦可使用 has got 的縮讀形式（**'s got**），但是只有主詞是**代名詞**（**we、you、they**）而不是名詞的情況下，才能使用 have got 的縮讀形式（**'ve got**）：

- John**'s got** an appointment.
- My dad**'s got** an old guitar.

NOT ~~The boys've got a football.~~

FAQ

Q: 我可以用沒有 **got** 的縮讀形式嗎？例如說 I've no money？

A: 可以，但這個用法不適用於第三人稱單數，因為 has 的縮讀形式（'s）可能會與 be 的縮讀形式（is → 's）混淆。所以不能說 He's no money，而該說 He has no money 或 He's got no money。

Q: 我可以使用有 **got** 的完整形式嗎？例如說 I have got one ticket。

A: 當然可以，只是縮讀形式較為常見罷了。

動詞 have 用於表達「擁有」以下事物：

1 所有物：I've got a new car.
2 親屬：Simon's got a sister.
3 外觀特徵：She's got beautiful dark eyes.
4 疾病與傷勢：I've got a cold.

1 請以縮讀形式來改寫句子在筆記本上。

1 My mother has got a part-time job.
2 They have got some relatives in Australia.
3 My cousins have got a kitten.
4 You have got great talent!
5 My brother has got a degree in physics.
6 She has got a very large house.
7 We have all got black hair in my family.
8 Julie has got a fantastic voice.

2 請重新排序單字來造句。

1 has / hair / my / long, / straight / sister / .

....

2 got / bad / headache / I've / very/a / .

....

3 have / I / tattoo / left / on / arm / my / a / .

....

4 two / for / tickets / we've / concert / got / the / .

....

5 hotel / pool / has / our / an / got / indoor / .

....

6 dad / your / has / good / of / sense / humor / a / .

....

7 have / we / a / dog / black / big, / got / .

....

8 got / your / phone / I've / number / .

....

動詞 have 的其他意義

動詞 have 亦有「**做**」、「**取用**」、「**購買**」、「**吃**」或「**喝**」的意思。在此用法下，後面**不能接 got**。

- **have** breakfast/lunch/dinner/supper
- **have** tea/coffee/fruit juice
- **have** a snack/sandwich
- **have** a break/vacation
- **have** a rest/nap/lie-in

- **have** fun / a good time (= enjoy)
- **have** a party/meeting (= organize, arrange)
- **have** a walk / bike ride / boat trip (= go for . . .)
- **have** a bath/shower
  (美式 take a bath/shower)

! 當我們想知道某人哪裡不對勁時，我們不會說「What have you got?」，而會說「What's the matter?」、「What's the matter with you?」或「What's wrong with you?」。

---

3 下方部分句子有誤。請在錯誤的部分**畫底線**並訂正。

1 Adam's spiky hair. ....

2 I've got a new coat. ....

3 She's got a shower every morning. ....

4 The children've blue eyes. ....

5 Dad's got a rest in the afternoon. ....

6 Have got a good time at the party! ....

7 They have milk and cereal for breakfast. ....

8 We often have lunch in a café. ....

LESSON 2 動詞have：否定句和疑問句
Verb have — negative and interrogative forms

否定句

我們通常會以**縮讀形式**來表達否定句裡的動詞 have，並且會以 **got** 加強語氣（have not got → haven't got）。

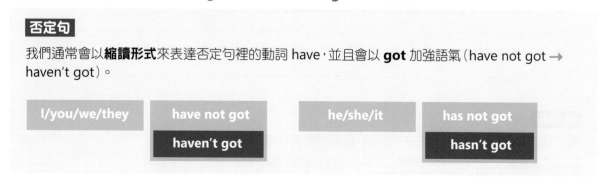

I/you/we/they	have not got
	haven't got

he/she/it	has not got
	hasn't got

Q: 我有一個美國朋友常說「I don't have a clue.」，為什麼不說「I haven't got a clue.」呢？

A: have 的否定也可以用 **don't have** 表示，其實這是最常見的美式英文用法。

! 當動詞 have 意思**不是**表「**持有**」時（請見上一頁所列的例子），否定句一定要使用 **don't** 以及單數第三人稱的 **doesn't**：
- I **don't have** a big breakfast in the morning.
- She **doesn't have** lunch at school.

---

1 請以 have got、has got、haven't got 或 hasn't got 來完成句子。

1 Rachel is blonde. She .... dark hair.

2 I usually cycle to school because I .... a car.

3 Their house .... a big garden with lots of flowers.

4 Melinda? No, she .... any children.

5 George .... long hair and he often ties it up in a pony tail.

6 They .... tattoos on their arms. I don't like them!

7 We .... a lot of books at home. We need to build some more shelves!

8 Bob .... two lovely dogs, but he .... any cats.

2 請在自己的筆記本裡，將以下句子改寫為否定句。

1 I've got some warm clothes with me.

2 She's got a present for you.

3 The students have a break at 11 o'clock in the morning.

4 He's got a lot of contacts on social media.

5 They have a vacation in July.

6 She usually has tea for breakfast.

7 My mother's got blue eyes.

8 We've got tickets for the match.

3 請使用提示用詞來造句。

0 Susan / country house (✗) / apartment in the town center (✓)
  Susan hasn't got a country house, but she has got an apartment in the town center.
  ....

1 My bedroom / balcony (✗) / French windows (✓)
  ....

2 The village / a post office (✓) / a bank (✗)
  ....

3 I / trees in my garden (✗) / lots of flowers (✓)
  ....

4 We / enough money for a pizza (✗) / enough for a couple of sandwiches (✓)
  ....

疑問句

問句裡的動詞 have 必須放在主詞前面，且通常會搭配使用 got。

| Have I/you/we/they got . . . ? | Has he/she/it got . . . ? |

簡答句

簡答句的句型如下：

Yes, + 代名詞 + have/has.	**No**, + 代名詞 + haven't/hasn't.

肯定簡答句必須使用完整形式的動詞，**否定簡答句**則通常會使用縮讀形式。
注意簡答句永遠不能使用 got：

- "Have you got your tablet?" "Yes, I **have**."
- "Has Karen got a motorbike?" "No, she **hasn't**."

否定疑問句

1 否定疑問句通常用以**核實資訊**。

> **Haven't I/you/we/they got . . . ?**

> **Hasn't he/she/it got . . . ?**

- "**Haven't** you got your key?"
  "Yes, I have!"
- "**Hasn't** your mom got a sister?"
  "No, she hasn't."

2 當動詞 have 的意思不是表「持有」時，一定要使用 **do/does** 開頭的問句：
- **Do** you usually have a bath or a shower?

3 以**美式英文**而言，含有 **have**（包括「持有」意思在內）的所有問句，均使用以下句型：

> **Do you have . . . ? / Does he have . . . ?**

- **Do you have** a new email address?

4 問句也能用 Wh 疑問詞開頭（如 what、where、when、why 等）：
- **Why** have you got that big smile on your face?
- **What** do we have to eat?

---

4 請將 **1–6** 的問句和 **A–F** 的答句配對。

1 Have you got any plans for tonight?
2 Has Ben got any good video games?
3 It's heavy! What have you got in your bag?
4 Have we got time to catch the next train?
5 Have you got any good music on your MP3 player?
6 Have you got any pink clothes?

A My clothes and a lot of books.
B Yes, but we must hurry.
C No. I hate pink!
D No, I haven't. Have you got any ideas?
E Yes, he has. I sometimes borrow them.
F Yes, I have. Lots of rock and pop.

1 ..... 　 2 ..... 　 3 ..... 　 4 ..... 　 5 ..... 　 6 .....

5 請將第 4 大題的問句，改寫為美式英文用法。

1 Do you have any plans for tonight? ....
2 ....
3 ....
4 ....
5 ....
6 ....

6 請根據下方提示用詞，搭配 have got 寫出肯定句、否定句與疑問句。

1 My house / solar panels on the roof. ....
2 I / not / time to chat. I'm busy at the moment. ....
3 "Peter / a big family/?" "Yes, he / four children." ....
4 "What car / you/?" "I / a hybrid car. It's very cheap to run."

....

5 London / a population of over 8.3 million. ....

6 We/not / much money. We must find an ATM. ....

7 "you / any preferences for your room?" "I'd like a non-smoking one, please."

....

8 "your school / a big playground / ?" "No, but it / a very big gym."

....

9 "you / any hand luggage, madam/?" "I / only this handbag."

....

10 We / not / any bread / but / we / some breadsticks.

....

LESSON 3 所有格形容詞/所有格代名詞 Possessive adjectives and pronouns

所有格形容詞如下：

my name 我的	**our** names 我們的
your name 你的	**your** names 你們的
his name 他的	**their** names 他們的
her name 她的	
its name 它的	

所有格形容詞有以下特點：

❶ 不會隨著名詞的性別或單複數而跟著改變：

my father │ **my** mother │ **my** brothers │ **my** sisters

❷ 前面不能直接加冠詞、指示形容詞（如 this、that）或不定形容詞（如 some、all）等任何限定詞：

- **our** school NOT ~~the our school~~
- this friend of mine NOT ~~this my friend~~
- a cousin of mine / one <u>of</u> **my** cousins NOT ~~a my cousin~~
- some books of yours / some <u>of</u> **your** books NOT ~~some your books~~

❸ 在單數第三人稱的部分，所有格形容詞指的是**持有者的身分**：

- **Tony's** office → **his** office（陽性） • **Sandra's** office → **her** office（陰性）
- **the bird's** cage → **its** cage（中性，用於動物和事物）

> **!** 請小心分辨下方的例子：
> - **You're** a friend. 不等於 **Your** friend . . . • **He's** a friend. 不等於 **His** friend . . .
> - **It's** a nice photo. 不等於 **Its** photo . . .

❹ 有時我們會以 **own** 來強調所有格形容詞：

- Each shop has got its **own** brand.（強調「店自己的」品牌）
- Was it his **own** idea?（強調「他自己的」點子）

Focus

英文的所有格形容詞，亦有下列搭配用法：

❶ 身體部位：
- I've broken **my** leg.
- She writes with **her** left hand.

❷ 衣物：
- Take **your** coat!
- He's wearing **his** black jeans.

1 請將 1-6 句中的主詞圈出來，與 A-G 的句子配對，並圈出對應該主詞的所有格形容詞。

<u>C</u> **0** (I)'m Tom, the new waiter.

..... **1** So you're from Pakistan.

..... **2** Zimbabwe is an African country.

..... **3** Mr. Johnson's our math teacher.

..... **4** Kate is my best friend.

..... **5** We live in a high building.

..... **6** My uncle and aunt like traveling

A Its capital is Harare.

B in their camper van.

C (My) surname's Brown.

D Our apartment's on the eighth floor.

E Is Urdu your mother tongue?

F Her brother Ben is at college.

G His tests are always very difficult.

2 請使用正確的所有格形容詞來完成句子。

1 The boys have .... own room.

2 What do you have in .... hand?

3 That building has a big dish on .... roof.

4 Is she wearing .... hat with the flowers on it?

5 Oh no! I don't have .... sunglasses.

6 He still can't stand on .... own two feet!

7 We've come in .... own car.

8 What are .... names, girls?

3 以下句子均有一個錯誤，請找出並訂正。

1 The his house is on Darwin Road. ....

2 Emma's got a little brother. He's name's Harry. ....

3 This farm belongs to my grandparents. It's your farm. ....

4 She's wearing his new red dress. ....

5 The hamster isn't in our cage! ....

6 My diary has got flowers on it's cover. ....

7 I often have sleepovers at the my friend's house. ....

8 John and Simon have his own fitness instructor. ....

9 Karen's got a sister. She's name is Davina. ....

所有格代名詞

❶ 所有格代名詞與所有格形容詞相同，不會隨著名詞的性別或單複數改變，且前面永遠不能加上限定詞：

my → **mine**	his → **his**	our → **ours**
your → **yours**	her → **hers**	their → **theirs**

❷ 當句子裡沒有相對應的名詞時，就使用**所有格代名詞**，如「It's **mine**.」。

❸ 我們可用**所有格形容詞 + own** 來替換代名詞：Is it **yours**? → Is it **your own**?

4 請圈出正確的用字。

1 Don't touch. They're not **your** / **yours**!

2 Give me **your** / **yours** cell phone number and I'll give you **my** / **mine**.

3 This isn't Mark's notebook. **His** / **Hers** has got a red cover with **his** / **her** initials on it.

4 They've got an Audi, so that Mercedes certainly isn't **ours** / **theirs**.

5 I think this bag belongs to Fran. Yes, I'm sure it's **her** / **hers**.

6 My boyfriend's coming to the party tonight. What about **yours** / **your**?

7 My parents' house is opposite the station and **our** / **ours** is behind it.

8 About half of smartphone users check **their** / **theirs** phones several times an hour.

LESSON 4 Whose 疑問詞與所有格
Interrogative *Whose* and the possessive case

❶ Whose 用在詢問物品**持有人**的問句，可以當作形容詞或是代名詞：
- **Whose** cell phone is this?（當形容詞）/
  Whose is this cell phone?（當代名詞，但注意此句式並不常用）

❷ Whose 問句可以用以下方式回答：
- ❶ 持有人的姓名 + **'s**：It's **Olivia's**.
- ❷ 所有格形容詞：It's **her** cell phone.
- ❸ 所有格代名詞：It's **hers**.

1 請重新排序單字，寫出兩種不同問句。

0 socks / are / these / whose / ?　　　Whose socks are these?

1 scooters / those / whose / are / ?　　..

2 is / coat / that / whose / ?　　　..

3 is / whose / number / telephone / this / ?　..

4 are / suitcases / whose / those / ?　..

5 this / whose / magazine / is / ?　　..

6 that / whose / is / idea / ?　　　..

2 請將下方答句與第 **1** 大題的問句配對。

..0.. They're David's socks.

...... Does it finish with double eight? It must be John's.

...... The blue scooter is my brother's. The other one belongs to his friend.

...... I don't know. No one has claimed them so far.

...... Which one? The brown leather coat? It's Mark's.

...... It's her idea! What do you think? Is it good?

...... It's not mine. I don't read stuff like that. Someone left it on the seat.

Focus

❶ 當所有格用於表達「持有」的意義時，寫作： 持有人的姓名 + **'s** + 被持有物 （注意不加冠詞！）：
- Adam**'s** car

❷ 切記，英文裡的**持有人姓名**，一定要放在**持有物的前面**：
- my daughter**'s** school

❸ 所有格亦可用於表達**親屬關係**：
- my mother**'s** cousin　　　• your sister**'s** husband

---

❶ 持有人是**字尾 s** 的規則複數名詞時，我們最後僅加上撇號：
- my parents**'** bedroom　　　• the Students**'** Union

　但請注意是 the children**'s** toys （字尾不是 s 的不規則複數名詞）

❷ 持有人是**字尾 s** 的單數人名時，我們通常會加 **'s**：
- James**'s** friend　　　• Charles**'s** car

❸ 但如果是名人的名字或姓氏，我們通常僅加撇號（請參見第 75 頁）。

擁有相同物品的持有人超過兩人時，我們僅會在後者人名加 **'s**：

- Sheila and Frank**'s** room
- Tom and James**'s** video games
（表示這兩位男孩共同持有這個電玩遊戲）

但請注意 Tom's and James's video games 是表示兩位男孩各有自己的電玩遊戲。

持有者具備以下性質時，需使用所有格：

1 人物或動物：
- Sarah**'s** garden
- the bird**'s** cage

2 意指人物的不定代名詞：
- no one**'s** land
- someone**'s** bag

3 團體：
- the band**'s** name
- the company**'s** headquarters

4 時間用語：
- a week**'s** holiday
- today**'s** newspaper
- tomorrow**'s** weather forecast
- an hour**'s** walk

5 地點名稱：
- London**'s** traffic
- the world**'s** top insurance company
- Chicago**'s** tallest building

不過，論及**由兩個名詞構成的某事物**時，後面不需要加 **'s**，而是將第一個名詞當作形容詞的用法：
- the **state** capital
- the **US** President（請參閱第 386 頁）

此外，我們還能使用介系詞 **of** 來表達：
- the pages **of** the book
- the lid **of** the pan

3 請使用所有格來改寫<u>畫底線</u>的單字。

0 We're reading <u>the plays of Ibsen</u> in our literature lessons. ....Ibsen's plays.............

1 I'm having <u>a vacation of a week</u> next month. ....

2 Can I have <u>the email address of your brother</u>, please? ....

3 I'm not allowed to go into <u>the bedroom of my brothers</u>. ....

4 I think this is <u>one of the best songs of Amy Winehouse</u>. ....

5 <u>The tricks of the clowns</u> are quite funny. ....

6 I love <u>the paintings of Van Gogh</u>! ....

7 <u>The office of the principal</u> is on the first floor. ....

4 請以兩個名詞放在一起的形式，改寫為較簡短的表達方式。

0 the lessons of math → ......the math lessons......................

1 the walls of the kitchen	**4** the cover of the book	**7** the screen of the computer
....	....	....
2 the charger of the laptop	**5** the handle of the door	**8** the remote control of the TV
....	....	....
3 the cap of the pen	**6** the legs of the table	**9** the top of the tree
....	....	....

5 請使用所有格來改寫句子。

0 Jenny has an Alsatian dog.　　　Jenny's dog ....is an Alsatian.............................

1 My mother has got a white bicycle.　　My mother's ....

2 This computer belongs to my father.　　It's ....

3 My girlfriend has got beautiful eyes.　　My girlfriend's ....

4 These backpacks belong to the guides.　These are ....

5 Kate's got a new smartphone.　　　Kate's ....

6 Charlie has a very good computer.　　Charlie's ....

FAQ

Q: 為什麼有些商店的名稱後方會有「's」？例如紐約的「Macy's」（梅西百貨）？

A: 這邊省略了 shop 或 store（商店），不寫出來讓大家自行理解意會。cathedral（天主教堂）、restaurant（餐廳）、salon（美髮沙龍）、surgery（外科診所）等地點名稱同樣會有此類用法，例如：
- We visited St Paul's.（意指 St Paul's Cathedral〔聖堡羅天主教堂〕）She's at the hairdresser's（意指 hairdresser's salon〔美髮師所屬的美髮沙龍〕）

Q: House 這個字也有這種可省略的用法嗎？

A: 有的，所以也可以說 I had a sleepover at Helen's（意指 Helen's house〔Helen 的家〕）。

---

6 請運用以下單字來完成句子。

| chemist's | doctor's | produce seller's | dentist's | baker's | Rino's | St. Peter's | my friend's |

1 Last night we had dinner at .... , a new Italian restaurant.

2 I'm going to the .... to buy some aspirin.

3 Did you go to .... when you were in Rome?

4 I don't feel very well. I must go to the ....

5 I spent the afternoon at .... We did our homework together.

6 Try the .... on Green Street. They bake great bread.

7 Why don't you go to the .... if you have a toothache?

8 I usually buy my vegetables at an organic .... near my house.

雙重所有格

不定冠詞（**a**、**an**）、數字（**two**、**three** . . .）、不定形容詞、不定代名詞（**some**、**many**、**a few** . . .）和指示形容詞（**this**、**that**、**these** . . .）後面皆不能直接加上所有格。在此情況下，我們會使用**雙重所有格**的結構，也就是結合介系詞 **of** 和所有格 **'s**：

- a friend **of** Tom**'s** / one **of** Tom**'s** friends (NOT a̶ ̶T̶o̶m̶'̶s̶ ̶friend)
- some photos **of** Janet**'s** / some **of** Janet**'s** photos (NOT s̶o̶m̶e̶ ̶J̶a̶n̶e̶t̶'̶s̶ photos)
- three books **of** the children**'s** / three **of** the children**'s** books (NOT t̶h̶r̶e̶e̶ ̶c̶h̶i̶l̶d̶r̶e̶n̶'̶s̶ books)
- this movie **of** Spielberg**'s** (搭配指示形容詞時，這是唯一可用形式 NOT t̶h̶i̶s̶ ̶S̶p̶i̶e̶l̶b̶e̶r̶g̶'̶s̶ ̶movie)

---

7 請使用雙重所有格來改寫句子裡畫底線的部分。記得維持原句的意義。

0 A sister of Brenda moved to Germany last year. .....One of Brenda's sisters.....

1 Two neighbors of the Smiths' come from Pakistan. ....

2 A colleague of my brother is coming to visit us. ....

3 Many selfies of John's are on Facebook. ....

4 A friend of the Browns' is a very good golf player. ....

5 Four birthday presents of my cousin's were baseball caps! ....

6 A cousin of Peter's is moving to Canada. ....

7 Some stamps of my father's collection are very rare. ....

8 請看以下血緣關係樹狀圖，並使用所有格來表達親屬關係，以完成句子。

Joe ─┬─ Alice

Albert ─┬─ Maddie   Daphne ─┬─ Jack
        Ann   Mark

1 Mark is .... nephew.
2 Alice is .... mother.
3 Albert is .... son.
4 Ann is .... daughter.
5 Maddie is .... daughter-in-law.
6 Mark is .... grandson.
7 Joe is .... father-in-law.
8 Joe and Alice are .... grandparents.
9 Albert is .... husband.
10 Daphne is .... wife.

9 本大題有七個句子有誤，請找出錯誤並訂正。

1 The produce seller's near my house sells very nice fruit. ....
2 I usually have two week's vacation in July. ....
3 If you go to London, you must visit St. Paul's. ....
4 Where are the childrens' backpacks? ....
5 Is James's brother a friend of Thomas? ....
6 This isn't today's newspaper. It's yesterdays'. ....
7 I'm going to Peggy's to study history this afternoon. ....
8 Two UK's top attractions are the Tower of London and Windsor Castle. ....
9 My office is five minute's walk from the bus station. ....
10 The team's new coach is Mr. Russel. ....
11 One man's heaven is another man's hell. (Proverb) ....
12 *Knockin' on Heaven's Door* is a Bob Dylan's most famous songs. ....

10 請運用以下單字或片語，來完成句子。

your father's house	bicycles some of	Peter's and John's students'	girlfriend Mary and Lucy's	Mrs. son	car one of

1 .... Moulay is Bilal's mother.
2 This is my grandparents' old ....
3 Mr. Murray's .... is parked on the other side of the street.
4 Sarah is Tom's ....
5 That is the staff room and this is the .... cafeteria.
6 The children's .... are in the garage.
7 James is Sheila and Frank's ....
8 This is .... bedroom.
9 These are .... bedrooms.
10 Simon is .... Rick's best friends.
11 .... Brenda's photos are published on *National Geographic*.
12 That friend of .... is very nice.

ROUND UP 4

1 請運用下表單字，盡可能多寫出符合邏輯的句子在筆記本上。

主詞	動詞	受詞	其他補語
I We They Wimbledon Center Court Robert The black rhino That girl That man This mini-van A dice The Statue of Liberty	have has	big responsibilities three sons but no daughters a movable roof a new email address some chips a funny hat a gigantic horn a lot of homework a beard and a mustache six hundred names eight seats six faces a torch	in my new job in our packed lunch for tomorrow in my contact list in her hand

2 請使用簡單現在式的 be 動詞或 have 來完成以下短文。

Steve ¹............. married and ²............. two children, a boy and a girl. The boy,
Jimmy, ³............. 12 years old and the girl, Christine, ⁴............. ten.
Steve ⁵............. the manager of a big computer shop in town, while his wife,
Barbara, ⁶............. a doctor at the local hospital. They ⁷............. a lovely house
in the center, not far from the shop and the hospital. The house ⁸.............
a fairly big back garden where they often ⁹............. barbecues with friends.
They ¹⁰............. a dog too, a golden retriever that loves running in the garden
and loves sleeping next to the fireplace in the living room even more.

3 請使用 have 和提示用詞來寫出否定句。
注意不能從頭到尾使用 **haven't/hasn't got** 的形式。

1 They / lunch / at home / on weekdays.

....

2 I / a new car. This is my old one.

....

3 Sheila / an umbrella / with her.

....

4 The company / a new sales manager.
Mr. Jones is still the Chief Buyer.

....

....

5 We / a sandwich / for lunch / on the weekend.

....

6 That man / a pass. Stop him!

....

7 My parents / a walk / in the evening.
They're far too lazy.

....

....

8 I / a cold. Why are you asking?

....

9 Mark / breakfast at home. He usually
goes to a café next to his office.

....

....

10 Oh dear! I / my wallet with me. Can you
lend me some money?

....

....

延伸補充

❶ 當動詞 **have** 的意義是「**取用**」、「**吃**」或「**喝**」而不是「**持有**」的時候，have 就等同**行為動詞**，因此亦有**進行式**的用法：
  • I**'m having** a cup of tea.　　英式　She**'s having** a shower.

❷ 在祈使句裡，have 具有**主動示意或打招呼**的意義：
  • **Have** a biscuit!　　• **Have** a nice day.

4 請閱讀以下句子，判斷 have 在每個句子的性質：如表示持有或親屬關係，請寫 **P**；如為行為動詞，請寫 **A**；如為主動示意，請寫 **O**；如為打招呼請寫 **G**。

.... **1** Have a cool drink! It's so hot today!

.... **2** That lady has a beautiful pearl necklace.

.... **3** Bye! Have a nice evening and don't come back too late.

.... **4** The apartment has two balconies overlooking the park.

.... **5** We're having a great time at the seaside. We won't be back till next week!

.... **6** Richard doesn't have a brother. He's an only child.

5 請根據對方的回覆，使用動詞 have 來寫出合適的問句、主動示意、邀請或打招呼的句子。

1 "..?"
"Yes. I always have a sandwich for lunch.

2 "..., sir."
"Thank you. I'm sure I'll enjoy staying in this hotel."

3 "...?"
"No, not measles. Gwen's got chicken pox."

4 "...?"
"I've got two sandwiches and an apple in my packed lunch."

5 "... ."
"Thank you. Your cookies are delicious, but I've already had a lot."

6 "...?"
"Yes, I am. I'm having a break after writing for two hours."

7 "Let's ...."
"No, please. Not a walk again! I'm really tired."

8 "...?"
"Not any more! How can I have a rest if you are around?"

6 請搭配使用 Whose 與合適的所有格形容詞或所有格代名詞，來完成以下對話。

1 **Ellen**　　Are you sure this is [1].............. umbrella, Brad?

Brad　　Yes, it must be [2].............. . It's red and blue, exactly like [3].............. . [4].............. else could it be?

Ellen　　Well, it could be Sara's. [5].............. is also red and blue and it's near [6].............. desk.

Brad　　But Sara's not here today. And anyway it's raining, so I'll take it.

2 **Receptionist**　　Can I have [7].............. passports, Mrs. and Mr. Smith?

Mrs. Smith　　Here you are. This is [8].............. and this is [9].............. .

Receptionist　　Thanks. And this is [10].............. key. Are those suitcases [11]..............?

Mrs. Smith　　No, they're not [12].............. . [13].............. luggage is still in the car. Could you send a porter, please? This is [14].............. car key.

Receptionist　　Sure. Which is [15].............. car?

Mrs. Smith　　The green Jaguar just outside the door.

7 每個句子都有一個錯誤。請以<u>底線</u>標出錯誤並訂正。

1 Has Pat usually a snack during the break? ....

2 This is not mine tablet. It's Peter's. ....

3 Jason must be at home. That's her bicycle in the garden. ....

4 Don't wait for me. I'm going to the dentists' and I'll be back late. ....

5 Let's print the students's reports before the end of the lesson. ....

6 Why don't we read a Dickens' novel this year, Miss Pearson? ....

7 "Whose those cars are?" "I don't know. But they're parked outside our house." ....

8 Some my friends are coming for dinner tonight. ....

8 請完成意義相近的句子。

1 Are you wearing one of your father's ties?
Are you wearing a .... ?

2 A nephew of mine is moving to Australia next month.
One .... to Australia next month.

3 They painted the walls of the kitchen bright yellow.
They painted the kitchen ....

4 A neighbor of my sister's has a beautiful German shepherd called Rex.
One .... called Rex.

5 Some toys of the children's are still in the garden. Let's pick them up before it starts raining.
Some of .... garden. Let's pick them up before it starts raining.

6 The room door was locked.
The door ....

7 James lives next to one of his best friends.
James lives next to a ....

8 Some of Thomas's neighbors are having a barbecue in the garden.
Some neighbors ....

9 請使用所有格形容詞和所有格代名詞，來完成短文。

We are visiting some friends of [1]........................... in Scotland next June. [2]........................... house in the Highlands is quite small but warm and comfortable. Doug is a teacher in the village primary school. Most of [3]........................... students are the children of farmers — called crofters in this region. [4]........................... wife Fyfa works at the local post office. [5]........................... is a part-time job because she needs to look after [6]........................... children. There are three of them, all under seven, and [7]........................... main occupation is running around [8]........................... granddad's croft. [9]........................... grandma is an excellent cook and makes lots of cakes for [10]........................... grandchildren.

10 請使用最合適的單字來完成句子。

1 I have a terrible toothache. I'm going to the .... this afternoon.

2 I always buy organic fruit and vegetables at the .... in the square.

3 Are you going to the ....? Can you buy some bread for me, please?

4 There's a .... on the corner, but we never go there because we're vegetarian.

5 I have flu. Could you please go to the .... and buy some paracetamol for me?

6 You must go to the .... Your hair is really too long.

延伸補充

雖然我們學過，一般人名即使是字尾 s，仍會以 's 來呈現所有格形式（Charles → Charles's）（請參閱第 68 頁）；但若**常見名人的名字**或**姓氏是字尾 s**，改成所有格時，只要加上**撇號**即可：

- Euripides（希臘悲劇三大家之一尤里皮底斯）→ Euripides' life
- Jesus（耶穌）→ Jesus' miracles
- Dickens（19 世紀小說家狄更斯）→ Dickens' novels

11 請運用括號裡的單字，搭配所有格來完成句子。

1 .... are collected in this volume. (Sophocles / plays)

2 We're all meeting at .... (St. James / Park)

3 Did you read .... ? (Dickens / biography)

4 The one on the left is .... (Prince Charles / residence)

5 Is this .... ? (Mr. Fox / desk)

6 .... is only 14. (Douglas / son)

Reflecting on grammar

請研讀文法規則，再判斷以下說法是否正確。

		True	False
1	動詞 have 的後面一定要接 got。		
2	動詞 have 有兩種現在式。		
3	否定句和疑問句裡有動詞 have 的情況下，我們絕對不能使用助動詞 do。		
4	「I haven't got breakfast in the morning.」是正確的句子。		
5	所有格形容詞的前面，可以加上指示形容詞和不定形容詞。		
6	在單數第三人稱的部分，所有格形容詞指的是持有者的身分。		
7	所有格代名詞的前面可以加上定冠詞。		
8	全部的所有格代名詞字尾都是 s，只有 mine 除外。		
9	「Whose house is this?」和「Whose is this house?」是同義的正確句子。		
10	「A friend of my husband's often has lunch with us.」是正確的句子。		

祈使句／簡單現在式／頻率副詞／時間用語／受格代名詞／連接詞
Imperatives, Present Simple, Adverbs of Frequency, Time Expressions, Object Pronouns, and Connectors

LESSON 1 祈使句 The imperative

	肯定句	否定句
第二人稱單數與複數	Turn right.	**Don't** turn left.
第一人稱複數	Let's turn right.	**Let's not** turn left.

第二人稱祈使句有以下規則：

❶ 第二人稱單數與複數的形式都相同。

❷ **肯定**祈使句使用的是**原形動詞**。若要加強語氣，我們可在句首加上 **do**：**Do** think about it!

❸ **否定**祈使句則需於動詞前面加上 **don't** 或 **do not**：**Don't** touch it!

第二人稱的祈使句的用法如下：

❶ **命令、指示或建議一或多人**：
Do this. / Don't do this.

❷ **有禮地提出要求**，此時會搭配 **please** 或 **will you**：
- **Come** here, please.
- **Take** the dog for a walk, will you?

❸ **邀請**：**Come** and **see** me tomorrow.

❹ **主動示意**：**Have** some chips.

❺ **祝願**：**Have** a good time!

第一人稱複數祈使句的句型則為：

肯定句	Let's (Let us) + 原形動詞
否定句	Let's not + 原形動詞（不太常用）

第一人稱複數祈使句通常用在**提出建議**時：
- **Let's** do something together.
- **Let's not** do this.

---

1 請圈出正確的用字。

1 Claire, **give** / **let's give** that pencil back to your friend.

2 Please, **sit** / **let's sit** down here, Ms. Pearson.

3 **Wait** / **Don't wait** here to be seated.

4 Here . . . **don't have** / **have** a cup of tea.

5 **Don't** / **Let's** go to the new store. It's great!

6 **Don't** / **Let's** even think of buying that necklace. It's too expensive.

7 **Enjoy** / **Let's enjoy** your vacation!

8 **Let's go** / **Let's not go** out tonight. It's too cold and wet.

---

2 請用以下動詞搭配肯定（+）或否定（–）祈使句，來完成句子。

| walk   remember   turn   write   sit   read   jump   be   tell   lie |

1 (+) .... down when the bus is moving and (–) .... up and down!

2 (–) .... in the sun at midday. You may get sunburned.

3 (+) .... down this street for about 50 meters and then (+) .... left.

4 (+) .... this novel during the summer and then (+) .... a review of it in about 300 words.

5 (–) .... anyone. It's a secret.

6 (–) .... late tomorrow and (+) .... to bring your equipment.

3 請以第一人稱複數的肯定（+）或否定（−）祈使句，搭配以下動詞來完成提出建議的句子。

buy　make　work　play　watch　have　go

1 (+) .... a cake for Mom's birthday.

2 (+) .... in groups to study for the exam.

3 (−) .... food here. It's really expensive. (+) .... to the market.

4 (−) .... this movie. I've already seen it and it isn't very good.

5 (+) .... another game. I want to win this time.

6 Aren't you hungry? (+) .... something to eat.

LESSON 2 簡單現在式 Present simple

→ 圖解請見P. 406–407

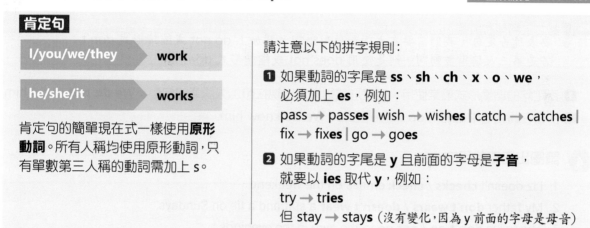

肯定句

I/you/we/they ➤ **work**

he/she/it ➤ **works**

肯定句的簡單現在式一樣使用**原形動詞**。所有人稱均使用原形動詞，只有單數第三人稱的動詞需加上 s。

請注意以下的拼字規則：

❶ 如果動詞的字尾是 **ss**、**sh**、**ch**、**x**、**o**、**we**，必須加上 **es**，例如：
pass → pass**es** | wish → wish**es** | catch → catch**es** |
fix → fix**es** | go → go**es**

❷ 如果動詞的字尾是 **y** 且前面的字母是**子音**，就要以 **ies** 取代 **y**，例如：
try → tr**ies**
但 stay → stay**s**（沒有變化，因為 y 前面的字母是母音）

1 請於各欄寫下對應的第三人稱單數動詞。

kiss	play	cry	study	do	wash	watch	mix	like
marry	prefer	tidy	find	pass	reply	ask	say	hurry

-s	-es	-ies

2 請依照例句的形式，使用不同主詞來造句。

0 I play volleyball.　Sara........................ plays volleyball, too. ....

1 I study Russian.　Thomas..

2 My sister goes to university.　I ....

3 I live in Manchester.　My cousin ....

4 My mother loves antique furniture.　I ....

5 She gets up at seven o'clock.　I ....

6 I miss my friends.　He ....

7 I watch a lot of TV.　My boyfriend ....

祈使句／簡單現在式／頻率副詞／時間用語／受格代名詞／連接詞

3 請運用括號裡的簡單現在式動詞，來完成句子。

1 Pippa .... her room every Saturday morning. (tidy)

2 Tom .... hockey three times a week. (play)

3 Dad always .... the car on the weekend. (wash)

4 Chris .... his homework in the evening. (do)

5 My brother .... to work early in the morning. (go)

6 David .... the bus nearly every morning. (miss)

7 Maria always .... on time. (arrive)

8 She often .... up late in the evening. (stay)

否定句

I/you/we/they	**don't work**	he/she/it	**doesn't work**

❗ 要表達否定句，我們需要在主詞和原形動詞之間加上 do not 或縮讀形式 don't；若是第三人稱單數動詞，則是使用 does not 或縮讀形式 doesn't。

❶ 否定句的縮讀形式最常使用，完整形式則通常出現在想加強語氣的句型：We **do not** know him.

❷ 即使在肯定句中也能用 do 來強調語氣：We **do** know him.

4 請圈出正確的用字。

1 Liz doesn't **checks** / **check** emails on the weekend.

2 My father **don't wears** / **doesn't wear** a suit and a tie on Sundays.

3 The twins **don't go** / **not go** to the gym in the evenings.

4 My brothers **don't study** / **not study** after dinner.

5 Danny **gets not** / **doesn't get** up early on Sunday mornings.

5 請改寫為否定句。

1 Frances dances very well.

....

2 She likes romantic novels.

....

3 We have lunch at school.

....

4 They work in a hospital.

....

5 Catherine plays the violin.

....

6 We go shopping on Mondays.

....

7 The movie starts at 9:00.

....

8 He goes to work by car.

....

6 請使用 don't 或 doesn't 搭配以下動詞來完成句子。

| go (x2)   watch   work (x2)   play   have |

1 James .... breakfast.

2 My sister works in an office. She .... to university.

3 Rosie .... tennis.

4 My parents .... often .... TV in the evening.

5 I .... in a shop. I'm a vet, so I work in a surgery.

6 "You .... to work on Saturdays, right?" "Yes, that's right. I .... on weekends."

疑問句與簡答句

| Do I/you/we/they work? | • Yes, I/you/we/they do. • No, I/you/we/they don't. |
| Does he/she/it work? | • Yes, he/she/it does. • No, he/she/it doesn't. |

1 在**問句**句型裡，**do** 或 **does** 要放在主詞和原形動詞的前面。在簡答句的句型裡，我們會使用 **Yes** 或 **No**，後面接上主格代名詞，以及肯定或否定形式的助動詞 do/does。

2 在**否定問句**的句型裡，我們會將 **don't** 或 **doesn't** 放在主詞前面：
- **Don't you** like this painting?
- **Doesn't Tom** work with you?

3 Wh 疑問詞所構成的問句句型如下：

> **Wh 疑問詞 + do/does + 原形動詞 + ?**

- **Where do** you live?
- **What does** he want?
- **When do** they start work?

祈使句／簡單現在式／頻率副詞／時間用語／受格代名詞／連接詞

7 請以 do/does 完成問句，並寫出簡答句。

1 .... you have free wi-fi?
Yes, ...

2 .... Mark live near the school?
No, ...

3 .... the children like the zoo?
Yes, ...

4 .... your father speak Spanish?
Yes, ...

5 .... you and your friends go jogging every day?
Yes, ...

6 .... she play a musical instrument?
No, ...

7 .... you know the password?
No, ...

8 .... they like going to parties?
No, ...

8 請重新排序單字來寫出問句。

1 do / When / you / do / homework / your / ?
....

2 does / Where / come / your best friend / from / ?
....

3 music / What / of / kind / do / like / they / ?
....

4 does / How much / that / cost / smartphone / ?
....

5 Which / do / like / you / song / best / ?
....

6 have / you / What / do / breakfast / for / ?
....

9 請將第 8 大題的問句與下方答句配對。

☐ **A** I have yogurt and fruit.

☐ **B** They like heavy metal.

☐ **C** We usually do it in the evening.

☐ **D** I prefer the first one.

☐ **E** He comes from the Philippines.

☐ **F** About $100.

10 請根據答句內容，完成對應的問句。

1 "What .... on Sundays?" "We usually get up at 9:00."

2 "How ....?" "I go to work by car."

3 "Who .... Michael .... with the housework?" "His mom."

4 "Where ....?" "I usually meet my friends at the park."

5 "When .... abroad?" "I go abroad in the summer. We have a house in Spain."

6 "Why .... with her grandparents?" "Because her parents are in Dubai at the moment."

79

簡單現在式的用法

簡單現在式適用於以下情況：

❶ **固定時間**；例如交通運輸工具的到站與離站時間、公司營業與關門時間，以及活動的起迄時間：
  • The train **leaves** at 7:35 and **arrives** at 9:25.

❷ **習慣性的行為**：
  • I usually **check** my emails in the evening.

❸ **永遠屬實的事實**，包括科學和宇宙方面的真理法則：
  • The sun **rises** in the east.

❹ **當前不會改變的情況**，例如某人的居住地或職業：
  • I **live** in Italy, but I **work** in Switzerland.

FAQ

Q: 我是一個商店助理，但我的聘僱合約有時間限制，因此不是一份永久職務。當我聊到此情況時，仍應使用簡單現在式嗎？

A: 如果你清楚表示這是**暫時性**的狀態，就應該使用現在**進行式**，如：「I'm working as a shop assistant. I'm living at my cousin's.」並可於最後加上 at the moment（請參閱第 94-95 頁）。

簡單現在式搭配的動詞，亦常用於表達以下情況：

❶ **喜好**（like、love、prefer、hate）
  • I **like** rap, but he **prefers** jazz.

❷ **心理認知**（know、remember、understand、mean）
  • I **don't know** what you mean.

❸ **意願**（want、wish）
  • I **want** to go home.

❹ **表達看法、贊同與否**
  （think、believe、agree、disagree）
  • What **do** you **think**?

❺ **持有**（own、belong、have）
  • My family **owns** and runs a **small** restaurant.

❻ **感官**（feel、sound、look、smell）
  • This cake **looks** nice. And it **smells** nice, too.

11 請判斷句子是否正確，正確請打勾 ✓，錯誤請打叉 ✗，並且訂正錯誤的句子。

1 Water freeze at 0°C and boil at 100°C. ....

2 The museum closes at 6:00 p.m. ....

3 The match doesn't starts at three o'clock. ....

4 This laptop don't belongs to the teacher. ....

5 What you think of this plan? ....

6 Her voice sounds weak tonight. ....

7 I doesn't agree with you. ....

8 Sam hates going shopping. ....

9 Do they want to eat out tonight? ....

10 He doesn't believes his team can win today. ....

11 Does he wants to go to the movies with us? ....

12 The Earth takes 365 days to go around the Sun. ....

LESSON 3 頻率副詞／時間用語 Adverbs of frequency and expressions of time

頻率副詞

為了表達某行為有多常發生，我們會使用頻率副詞：

always
usually
often
sometimes
occasionally
seldom/rarely
never

always	usually	often	sometimes	occasionally	seldom/rarely	never
100%	80%	60%	30%	20%	10%	0%

頻率副詞的位置

簡單現在式搭配頻率副詞的句型如下：

肯定句：主詞 + **副詞** + 動詞

- I **never** use my car to go to work.
- I **always** take the bus.

> **!** 不過，在有 **be 動詞**的句子裡，
> 副詞需放在 **be 動詞**後面：
> I am **always** hungry at this
> time of day.

否定句：主詞 + **don't/doesn't** + **副詞** + 動詞

- I don't **usually** get up late on Sundays.

疑問句：

(Wh 疑問詞) + **do/does** + 主詞 + **副詞** + 動詞 + ?

- When do you **usually** have a break?
- Do you **ever** come to this hotel?

UNIT 5

FAQ

Q: 我常聽到「I go to concerts sometimes.」之類的句子，或是「Sometimes I go to concerts.」，但不是應該說「I sometimes go to concerts.」嗎？

A: 三種句子都對。
sometimes 屬於「位置自由」的副詞，因此可放在句首或句尾。

---

1 請改寫句子，將副詞放在正確位置。

1 We meet for a drink after work. (occasionally)
....

2 My brother is at home in the evening. (never)
....

3 Where do you have lunch? (usually)
....

4 He listens to classical music. (sometimes)
....

5 I don't go to the theater. (often)
....

6 They are at school in the morning. (always)
....

7 My friend eats meat. (rarely)
....

8 We see each other on weekends. (never)
....

2 請在句中加入頻率副詞，來符合你做這些事情的頻率。

1 I go to the market on Saturday morning. ....

2 I am at home in the mornings. ....

3 I play tennis on the weekend. ....

4 I sleep till late on Sunday morning. ....

5 I go to the theater with my friends. ....

3 請重新排序單字來造句。

1 seldom / They / piano / lessons / have / in / morning / the / . ...
2 often / Internet / surfs / the / Greg / in / evening / the / . ...
3 This / is / train / time / on / usually / . ...
4 Mom / Does / come / late / from / back / ever / work / ? ....
5 sometimes / Jill / works / on / weekend / the / . ...

How often 問句與時間片語

要回答「How often . . . ?」問句，我們可以使用**頻率副詞**，或以下表達頻率的**時間片語**：

- every day/week/month
- on Saturdays/Sundays
  （以此例來說，在星期六／日的後面加 s，意指每一個星期六／日）
- on the weekend

once		
twice		a day/month/year
three/four times		

此類時間用語，通常會放在**句尾**：

- "How often do you have a piano lesson?"
  "I have a piano lesson **once a week**, on Tuesday afternoon."

---

4 請將問句和答句配對。

1 Do you ever play sports during the week?
2 Does the supermarket open before eight?
3 How often do you go to the movies?
4 How often does Dan come back from college?
5 When do you usually visit your grandparents?
6 Do you ever sleep in on Sunday mornings?

A Yes, but only on Wednesday mornings when it opens at 7:30.
B Every weekend! He's quite lucky.
C About once a month, but I watch lots of movies on TV.
D Yes, quite often, especially in winter.
E Yes, I train with my team twice a week.
F On Sundays. We often have lunch together.

1 ..... 　 2 ..... 　 3 ..... 　 4 ..... 　 5 ..... 　 6 .....

---

5 請使用下表的單字，寫下至少六個符合邏輯的問句。

Where How much How What time When How often	do does	these shoes the post office the yoga 　　course your parents the bus this book this machine you the shops	stop? leave? cost? work? open? start? practice? close?

1 ....
2 ....
3 ....
4 ....
5 ....
6 ....
7 ....

---

6 請如例句所示，以表達頻率的時間用語，取代畫底線的單字。

0 Matt works out in the gym <u>on Tuesdays and Thursdays</u>. → twice a week

1 I go to school <u>from Monday to Friday</u>. ....

2 We go to the beach <u>in July and September</u>. ....

3 My parents go on a cruise <u>in May</u>. ....

4 I meet my friends <u>on Monday, Tuesday, Wednesday, Thursday, Friday, Saturday and Sunday</u>. ....

5 Take these tablets <u>in the morning and in the evening</u>. ....

6 We get our school report <u>in January, June and December</u>. ....

7 We have a math test <u>on the 4th, 10th, 16th and 27th of each month</u>.

....

LESSON 4 受格代名詞／連接詞 Object pronouns and some conjunctions

主詞	I	you	he	she	it	we	you	they
	↓	↓	↓	↓	↓	↓	↓	↓
受詞	me	you	him	her	it	us	you	them

受格代名詞的位置如下：

❶ 放在**動詞**後面：
• Why don't **you** love me?

❷ 放在 with、for、to、at 等**介系詞**後面：
• I want to be with **you**.   • I'm waiting for **them**.

Focus

❶ 英文的受格代名詞和動詞一起念時，有時會因為連音而聽起來像是一個單字，但書寫時仍然是與動詞分開的兩個詞彙，如 tell him、give me。

❷ 注意英文的受格代名詞一定要放在**動詞後面**，如：「I know her.」。

1 請使用受格代名詞來完成句子。

1 I like that jacket. Do you like ....?

2 Those jeans are nice. I want to try .... on.

3 We're going home now. Are you coming with ....?

4 "Are you writing to Tom?" "No, I'm not writing to ...."

5 Look! That's Angela. Let's call ....

6 Here's a present for .... , Louise. Happy birthday!

7 Peter and Bev? I'm going to meet .... at the pub right now.

8 I'm going shopping in a minute. Do you want to come with .... ?

2 請重新排序單字來造句。

1 talking / Are / to / you / me / ?
....

2 present / Here's / a / you / , / Dad / for / !
....

3 her / I / know / very / don't / well / .
....

4 like / I / very / it / much / .
....

5 They / us / are / with / coming / .
....

6 for / Can / please / wait / you / me / , / ?
....

3 請以主格代名詞或受格代名詞，來取代**畫底線**的名詞。

1 <u>Lucy</u> is going to meet <u>her uncle</u> at the airport. ....

2 Do you want to play with <u>me and my friend</u>? ....

3 Give <u>this notebook</u> to Sarah, please. ....

4 <u>John</u> wants to buy <u>this T-shirt</u>. ....

5 Who's going with <u>Harry</u>? <u>Harry</u>'s got a big car. ....

6 Listen to <u>your mother</u>! <u>Your mother</u>'s probably right. ....

7 Where are <u>my glasses</u>? I can't find <u>my glasses</u>. ....

8 Can you meet <u>my friends</u> at the station? <u>My friends</u> are arriving at 2:00. ....

祈使句／簡單現在式／頻率副詞／時間用語／受格代名詞／連接詞

4 請圈出正確的用字。

1 Please stop here **because / so / and** that's my house.

2 They like studying together **because / so / but** they meet at my house every day.

3 I usually take a shower in the morning **but / and / or** then I have breakfast.

4 Can you make me a cup of tea **so / or / but** a hot chocolate, please?

5 Do your math homework now **so / or / but** we can go out later.

6 We often watch a movie **but / so / or** a quiz show after dinner.

7 Do you really want to have both chocolate cake **or / and / so** ice cream?

8 Don't sit on that chair **so / but / because** it's broken!

5 請以合適的連接詞完成句子。

1 I sometimes have bacon .... eggs for breakfast.

2 Gary plays baseball, ... he can't play basketball.

3 We're late, ... we'd better take a taxi.

4 We can go to the movies .... stay at home .... watch a video.

5 Let's meet at 3:00 .... 3:30. What time is best for you?

6 Fish .... chips is typical English street food.

7 We can't visit the museum now .... it's closed on Mondays.

8 I'm putting on weight, ... I want to go on a diet.

6 請以合適的連接詞，合併兩個句子。

0 My friends have a beautiful house. They also have big garden.

My friends have a beautiful house and a big garden.

1 Go to the science lab quickly. Your teacher is waiting for you.

....

2 Would you like an apple? Would you prefer an orange?

....

3 Come before five. We can have a nice chat this way.

....

4 Steve is a nice boy. He's a bit lazy.

....

5 My son helps me at home. He can't cook though.

....

7 請使用下列受格代名詞或連接詞來完成對話。

| them (x5)   him   me   because   and (x3)   so   or   but |

Sarah The German guys are arriving in two weeks' time for the school exchange, remember?

Sam Oh yes, that's right.

Sarah Are you going to host any of [1]........................... , Sam?

Sam Yes, I'm going to host a boy called Hans. I saw [2]........................... in a video he sent [3]........................... . What about you, Sarah?

Sarah No, I'm not hosting anyone [4]........................... we don't have a spare room, [5]........................... mine is too small for two beds.

Sam We are going to organize a welcome party for [6]........................... , aren't we, Sarah?

Sarah Sure. On Friday night. [7]........................... not at the school. We're going to have the party at the youth club.

Sam Great! [8]........................... who's going to meet [9]........................... at the airport?

Sarah I am. My dad's got a minibus [10]........................... we're going to drive [11]........................... to their host families' homes.

Sam Why don't we take [12]........................... bowling one night?

Sarah Good idea. [13]........................... we can go for a pizza [14]........................... to the movies another day.

8 請完成短文，空格內可以是主格和受格代名詞、所有格形容詞、連接詞或介系詞。

Liz doesn't like school much, [1]........................... she likes weekends! On Saturdays [2]........................... doesn't get up early [3]........................... she often stays out till late on Friday night. When she goes downstairs [4]........................... about ten, she makes [5]........................... own breakfast [6]........................... her parents usually go shopping in the morning. [7]........................... favorite shopping place is the big street market [8]...........................the main square, [9]........................... they leave home around nine and hardly ever come back before midday.

After breakfast, Liz phones her friends [10]........................... invites [11]........................... around for coffee. [12]........................... best friend Violet often stays for lunch too [13]........................... both her mother [14]........................... her father work all day on Saturday.

Violet [15]........................... Liz go out together in the afternoon, [16]........................... they don't go to the market; they prefer the big department store in the High Street. There they find [17]........................... favorite clothes and make-up, [18]........................... they don't always buy [19]........................... , they often only try [20]........................... on.

85

ROUND UP 5

延伸補充 與祈使句近義的表達方式

命令與禁令

祈使句	其他句型
Listen carefully!	You must listen carefully. It is important that you listen carefully. It is important for you to listen carefully. It is essential that you listen carefully.
Wait for me, please!	Can you please wait for me?
Don't cross here!	You mustn't cross here. / You can't cross here.
Don't enter!	No entry.
Don't smoke!	No smoking.
Don't fish!	No fishing.（常用於路標、告示）

建議、主動示意與提議

祈使句	其他句型
Don't be shy. Always try.	You shouldn't be shy. You should always try.
Have a cup of tea!	Will you have a cup of tea? Would you like a cup of tea? Do you want a cup of tea? / How about a cup of tea?
Let's go skating!	Why don't we go skating? / How about going skating? What about going skating? / Shall we go skating? （可參閱第 280 頁）

1 請以祈使句或上述不同片語來改寫出意義相近的句子。

1 You must always wear gloves and a mask.

....

2 You can't park your car here.

....

3 Will you have some coffee?

....

4 How about going to the leisure center?

....

5 Why don't we have an ice cream?

....

6 You should read this novel. It's really good.

....

7 It is important that you read the instructions before you start.

....

8 Why don't we talk about it?

....

9 You should never give up.

....

10 Can you please come here?

....

2 請將 **1–10** 與 **A–J** 配對，成為符合邏輯的完整句子。

1 Don't eat	**6** Carry your key	**A** the door of the fridge.	**F** immediately!
2 Always close	**7** Go	**B** with you at all times.	**G** on the pan.
3 Come here	**8** Please don't	**C** away!	**H** warm clothes. It's cold.
4 Put the lid	**9** Give it	**D** be angry!	**I** shouting!
5 Wear	**10** Stop	**E** all the cookies.	**J** back to me, please.

1 .....   **2** .....   **3** .....   **4** .....   **5** .....   **6** .....   **7** .....   **8** .....   **9** .....   **10** .....

3 判斷以下句子，如為命令請寫 **O**；如為禁令請寫 **P**；如為建議請寫 **A**；
如為主動示意請寫 **OF**；如為提議請寫 **S**。

.... **1** Don't touch the leaves of that plant. They are poisonous!

.... **2** I think you should be more optimistic.

.... **3** Why don't we drive to the coast on the weekend?

.... **4** Have a biscuit!

.... **5** Take the dictionary from the top shelf!

.... **6** Would you like something to drink?

.... **7** Let's walk to the station. It's a nice day!

.... **8** No fishing in this pond!

.... **9** Paul should be more active. He's too lazy.

.... **10** Do you want another blanket? It may be cold tonight.

.... **11** Read the instructions before using this appliance.

.... **12** Shall we visit the photo exhibition now?

4 請將交通路標與說明配對。

.... **1** Don't drive faster than 60 km/h.

.... **2** Give priority to vehicles from opposite direction.

.... **3** No overtaking.

.... **4** Motor vehicles aren't allowed in this street.

.... **5** You can't turn right.

.... **6** No U-turns.

.... **7** You can't stop here.

.... **8** Pedestrians only.

.... **9** No entry.

.... **10** No scooters.

5 請根據答句內容，寫出簡單現在式的 **Yes/No** 問句或 **Wh** 問句。

1 .... ?
Yes, I do. I have piano lessons every Monday.

2 .... ?
No, she doesn't. She never eats meat. She's vegetarian.

3 .... ?
Yes, they do. They spend a few days in the Alps every summer.

4 .... ?
I study Spanish as a foreign language.

5 .... ?
We have basketball practice three times a week.

6 .... ?
I prefer the blue dress.

7 .... ?
My sister works in a hospital. She's a nurse.

8 .... ?
My parents? They live in Canada.

9 .... ?
We often go jogging on the weekend.

10 .... ?
No, we hardly ever go to the theater because there isn't one in our little town.

11 .... ?
No, we never go to the mountains in summer.

12 .... ?
The Sales Manager's office? It's on the third floor.

13 .... ?
In the evening? My grandfather watches TV.

14 .... ?
We go to the movies once a week. We like it!

6 請使用以下單字來完成對話。

| can sign | you say | get me (x2) | give me |
| why don't you | go and see | turn down | |

Sarah Rob! I'm thirsty. [1].. a cola!

Rob Please.

Sarah [2].. a cola, please.

Rob Okay, lazy sister. Here you are.

Sarah The doorbell's ringing. Rob, [3].. who it is.

Rob It's DHL. A parcel for you.

Sarah I'm watching a movie. You [4].. for delivery.

Rob All right. Here's your parcel. Don't [5].. thank you?

Sarah Oh, yeah . . . [6].. the music, Rob! I can't hear the movie. And I hate that band!

Rob No, they're cool . . . Now, [7].. the remote. I want to watch the news.

Sarah [8].. watch the news on your tablet? I'm watching the TV.

Rob Sarah, you're horrible!

7 請以下列動詞的簡單現在式，來完成肯定句的對話內容。

catch (x2)   get up   say   work   go (x2)
finish   like   sleep   prefer

Dawn A proverb [1]........................... "The early bird [2]...........................
the worm." But you always [3]........................... till nine or ten in
the morning!

Matt And I still [4]........................... lots of worms! I'm an owl.
I [5]........................... working in the evenings and I always
[6]........................... to bed very late. The firm for which I
[7]........................... is quite flexible on working hours luckily.
The important thing is that I [8]........................... my work on time.

Dawn My brother is just like you. He usually [9]........................... after
nine and [10]........................... to bed at 1 or 2 a.m. But I
[11]........................... the early hours. I have a lot more energy
in the morning.

8 請以正確的主格代名詞和受格代名詞來完成對話。

Tom We love this band. Do you like [1]...........................?

Linda Yes, I do. I think [2]........................... are great.

Tom So why don't you go to the concert with Dave and [3]........................... next week?

Dave Come on. Join [4]...........................!

Linda Sorry, [5]........................... can't come to the concert with [6]........................... .
I'm working for my exam.

Tom Oh well, we'll tell [7]........................... all about it when we get back!

Reflecting on grammar

請研讀文法規則，再判斷以下說法是否正確。

		True	False
1	第一人稱複數的祈使句開頭為「Let's . . .」。		
2	第二人稱單數與複數，具有兩種不同形式的祈使句。		
3	所有人稱的簡單現在式，肯定句用法都相同。		
4	簡單現在式用於表達習慣性的行為，以及永遠屬實的情況。		
5	「He knows . . .」的否定句是「He doesn't knows . . .」。		
6	always 的反義詞是 never。		
7	肯定句的頻率副詞，通常放在動詞後面。		
8	代名詞 you 和 it 可身兼主格代名詞和受格代名詞。		
9	僅能以祈使句來下達命令。		
10	so 屬於引導結果的連接詞。		

動詞 ing 與現在進行式
V–ing Form and Present Continuous

LESSON 1 動詞ing *V–ing* form

❶ 我們所謂的動詞 ing，意指**現在分詞**或**動名詞**：
- I saw a man **walking** up and down the street.（意義與「the man was walking」相同）
- I bought a lot of stuff in the sales, **spending** very little money.
（意義與 and we spent 相同）

❷ 動詞 ing 通常是**原形動詞** + **字尾 ing** 而成：
- eat → eat**ing**
- look → look**ing**
- study → study**ing**
- play → play**ing**

請注意以下的拼字變化：

❶ 字尾 e 如果不發音，我們會去掉 e：
- hope → hop**ing**
- come → com**ing**

例外
- see → se**eing**
- be → b**eing**
（因為字尾 e 需要發音）

注意 有些動詞即使字尾 e 不發音，我們仍會保留，以避免混淆意思：dye → dy**eing**

❷ 如有以下情況，**字尾是子音**時，必須**重複一個子音再加 ing**：

❶ 單音節的動詞，而且單子音字尾的前面有一個母音：
- stop → stop**ping**
- sit → sit**ting**

例外
- beat → beat**ing**
- meet → meet**ing**（有兩個母音）
- send → send**ing**（有兩個子音）

❷ 雙音節的動詞裡，重音落在第二音節，且單子音字尾的前面有一個母音：
- refer → refer**ring**
- admit → admit**ting**

例外
- offer → offer**ing**（重音落在第一音節）
- repeat → repeat**ing**（第二音節有兩個母音）
- adopt → adopt**ing**（字尾有兩個子音）

❸ 字尾雙母音 ie 需改為 y：
- lie → l**ying**
- tie → t**ying**
- die → d**ying**

FAQ

Q: 我曾經打出「**traveling**」這個單字，結果電腦顯示拼字錯誤。為什麼會這樣？

A: 你的電腦很有可能是英式英文系統。traveling 是正確的美式英文拼法，但在英式英文裡，字尾「l」的動詞前面如果有一個母音，就需要重複「l」，因此要拼為 travelling。同理可證 counsel → counselling（英式英文）/counseling（美式英文）
例外：feel → feeling（兩個母音）

1 請將動詞改成 **ing** 的形式。

put	....	watch	....	leave	....
write	....	enter	....	answer	....
read	....	ask	....	lie	....
dance	....	hit	....	think	....
live	....	try	....	behave	....
stay	....	marvel (*Am.E.*)	....	work	....
transmit	....	commit	....	suffer	....
refer	....	wait	....	stop	....
dye	....	type	....	change	....
play	....	paint	....	copy	....
rise	....	get	....	shout	....

有字尾 **ing** 的單字，具有以下詞性：

❶ 當作動詞，搭配 be 動詞而構成進行式：
- It's **raining**.（請參閱下方 Lesson 2 內容）

❷ 當作形容詞：
- It's an **interesting** magazine.
- They're having an **exciting** vacation in the Caribbean

❸ 當作名詞，此時可作為句子的主詞，或是另一個動詞的受詞：
- **Swimming** is my favorite sport.（主詞）
- **Finding** a job is not easy.（主詞）
- I like **swimming**.（受詞）
- I hate **watching** horror movies.（受詞）

2 請將句子中的動詞 **ing** 畫底線。如作為動詞，請寫 **V**；如作為名詞，請寫 **N**；如作為形容詞，請寫 **A**。

..V.. **0** The children are <u>playing</u> video games as usual.

..... **1** Playing tennis is one of his favorite activities.

..... **2** I'm having a geography lesson in a few minutes.

..... **3** She really loves working out in the gym.

..... **4** Oh dear! That's such a heartbreaking story!

..... **5** We're leaving for Paris next week.

..... **6** That is shocking news.

..... **7** Congratulations! You're doing a really great job.

..... **8** Most people are interested in learning English.

3 請重新排序單字，寫出邏輯通順的句子。

1 is / Dad / exotic / cooking / an/meal / tonight / .

....

2 hobby / Knitting / is / favorite / Rachel's / .

....

3 I / drawing / enjoy / painting / and / .

....

4 performance / so / Her / disappointing / was / !

....

5 really / Japanese / is / challenging / Learning / .

....

6 moving / is / a / movie / This / deeply / .

....

LESSON 2 現在進行式 Present continuous

➜ 圖解請見P. 408–409

肯定句

現在進行式是用來說明講話當下、或在講話的前後期間正在發生的行為或事件：

- The boys and girls **are chatting** in the students' room.
- Mr. Reeds, the new customers **are waiting** in the hall.
- Susan **is working** a lot this week.

現在進行式的肯定句型如下：

I	am	
He/She/It	is	動詞 + ing
We/You/They	are	

由於現在進行式以 be 動詞構成，因此此時態同樣有縮讀形式，而且用法比完整形式更常見：

I'm	
He's/She's/It's/Jack's	動詞 ing
We're/You're/They're	

1 請將括號裡動詞改為現在進行式，來完成句子。

1 The students .... math exercises for tomorrow's test. (do)

2 Alice .... a nice T-shirt. (wear)

3 Tom .... breakfast right now. (have)

4 Some people .... in the street. (walk)

5 Kate .... TV. (watch)

6 John and Harry .... football in the park. (play)

7 Jasmine .... dressed for the party. (get)

8 I .... a text to my friend in the UK. (write)

9 We .... some food for tonight. (buy)

10 Mark .... his girlfriend. (text)

2 請以下列動詞的現在進行式來完成肯定句，並盡可能使用縮讀形式。

| stay   study   file   run   talk   lie   have **(x2)**   leave   work |

1 The secretary .... some documents.

2 My brother .... at San Francisco State University.

3 The President .... to Congress right now.

4 The students .... to their class because they're late.

5 The ship .... New York harbor.

6 We .... in the sun.

7 My friends .... at a four-star hotel by the sea.

8 I'm sorry. Ms. Sunis .... lunch at the moment. She can't talk to you right now.

9 Dad is busy right now. He .... dinner.

10 Sam .... on the roof. He can't talk to you on the phone.

否定句

現在進行式的否定句與 be 動詞的否定句相同：

| 主詞 | am/is/are | not | 動詞 ing |

否定句裡同樣常用**縮讀**形式：

- I'**m not** watching TV.
- He **isn't** playing with the children.
- We **aren't** leaving now.

- I'm sorry you **aren't** having a good time.
- They **aren't** working today.

3 請將第 2 大題的句子改寫為否定句，記得進行必要的文法變化。

1 ....

2 ....

3 ....

4 ....

5 ....

6 ....

7 ....

8 ....

9 ....

10 ....

4 請使用現在進行式，將單字組成否定句。

0 we / take / any photos
We aren't taking any photos.

1 Julie / read / a magazine
....

2 My parents / meet / their friends
....

3 You / study / history
....

4 They / drink / tea
....

5 Ben / play / football
....

6 I / go / to the park / this afternoon
....

7 They / file / documents
....

5 請以下列動詞的現在進行式來完成句子，可能是肯定句或否定句。

play (x2)　study (x2)　enjoy　go　cook　write　sleep　come

1 I .... math, I .... history because I have a test tomorrow.

2 Kate? No, she definitely .... tennis. She hates it.

3 The twins .... tonight — James is making the main course and Steve is making dessert.

4 I .... the party at all. I don't know anybody here, and the music is awful.

5 Can you turn down the music? The children ....

6 I .... on my computer! I .... really .... an email to my German key pal!

7 We .... to the movie theater tonight. Our friends .... for dinner and I'm cooking paella.

疑問句

現在進行式的疑問句與 be 動詞的疑問句用法相似。若是 Yes/No 問句，通常會搭配簡答句。

Are you going out?

- Yes, I am.
- No, I'm not.

Is he/she/it going out?

- Yes, he/she/it is.
- No, he/she/it isn't.

Are you/we/they going out?

- Yes, we/you/they are.
- No, we/you/they aren't.

Am/Is/Are + 主詞 + 動詞 ing + ?

- "**Are** you **cooking** dinner?" "Yes, I am."
- "**Is** Dan **coming** home late tonight?" "No, he isn't."

否定疑問句的句型如下：

Aren't/Isn't + 主詞 + 動詞 ing + ?

- **Aren't** they **working** this afternoon?
- **Isn't** Mom **having** a rest?

大家可從表格裡看出來，簡答句的句型與 be 動詞的簡答句完全一樣。(請參閱第 31 頁)

Wh 問句通常會將疑問詞放在 be 動詞前面：

疑問詞 + am/is/are + 主詞 + 動詞 ing + ?

- **What am** I **doing** here?
- **Why are** you **talking** so loud?

6 請將問句和答句配對。

1 What are the children doing?
2 Where's Jack posting his photos?
3 Why are you spending hours on your computer?
4 Why are they laughing so loudly?
5 What are you doing?
6 Are you playing offline?

A Because I'm looking for my old schoolmates.
B I'm chatting with my friend.
C No, I'm playing online.
D On all the social networks!
E They're playing upstairs.
F Because they're watching a funny movie.

1 .....　2 .....　3 .....　4 .....　5 .....　6 .....

7 請運用提示用詞，寫下現在進行式的問句和簡答句。

0 Paula / talk to Phil on the phone? (Yes.)
Is Paula talking to Phil on the phone?
....
Yes, she is.
....

1 your brother / sleep / on the sofa? (Yes.)
....
....

2 Jo and Tamsin / act / in the school play? (Yes.)
....
....

3 she / not watch / TV / tonight? (Yes.)
....
....

4 they / have breakfast / now? (No.)
....
....

5 Tom / not iron / his shirts? (No.)
....
....

6 you / not study / for your test tomorrow? (Yes.)
....
....

7 the train / leave / in ten minutes? (No.)
....
....

8 Rob / take part / in the tennis tournament? (Yes.)
....
....

8 請根據答句內容寫出問句。

0 Aren't you working today ....? Working? No, it's my day off.
1 ....? Staying at home? No, we're going for a walk this afternoon.
2 ....? Yes, we're going out. We're going to a concert.
3 ....? Yes, I am listening to my favorite rock band!
4 ....? Tom? No, I'm not chatting with him.
5 ....? Because we don't have any homework today, Mom.
6 ....? They're running because the train is leaving.
7 ....? I'm playing with my little sister.

現在進行式的用法

現在進行式用於針對**講話當下正在發生的行為**，此外還可用於以下情況：

❶ 講電話的時候：
• I'm studying right now, Ann. I can't chat with you.

❷ 描述景象或照片的時候：
• The person in the middle is sitting on a chair.